Early Praise

FRANKIE AND THE GIFT OF FANTASY

Mom's Choice Gold Award winner!

"A magical potion of fantasy and science, *Frankie and the Gift of Fantasy* is captivating and oh so charming, with its real boy and his escape/adventure to the creative, liberating planet of Urth. I can't wait for the rest of the series!"
—Cindy Conger, JustWrite Communications

"A beautiful and vivid world is created within these pages. The author does an absolutely phenomenal job of introducing the reader to the world at a rate that keeps the story magical. It's very similar to *Alice in Wonderland* in that way… This is an author I'll be keeping my eyes on."
—Lori Simmons, NetGalley reviewer

"Other quest and confrontation stories proceed in predictable manners. Not *Frankie and the Gift of Fantasy*. This lends it a unique, powerful voice that produces a standout in the genre of children's fantasy. The epic adventure flushes out Frankie and his family's concerns with the dilemmas of alien peoples who have as much at stake in Frankie's presence or absence as does his family back home."
—Midwest Book Reviews

"A gloriously inventive and profoundly sensitive adventure story of how young Frankie learns responsibility, compassion, empathy and, primarily, courage. Courage can certainly mean bravery in the face of physical danger. But it can also mean self-knowledge and an honest understanding of other people, with all their eccentricities, hopes and fears."
—Isabella Knight, Actor

"My daughter and I loved this book! We got lost in the world of Urth and Frankie's journey of self-discovery. We watched him spin stories and imagine worlds. Along the way Frankie evolves to use his imagination to be helpful, even selfless. We loved how Frankie found so many ways to use his imagination to overcome obstacles. By the end of the story, he learned that caring for others is just as important as caring for yourself."

—Lisa G., Nebraska

"An eye-opening and heart-warming story of a boy who discovers his strengths. An imaginative, fantastical rite of passage."

—Leslie Lange, soccer mom, Ventura, CA

"A dazzling adventure into the reaches of inner and outer space. A wonderful, valuable read for children."

—Angelica Kaner, PhD. Psychologist/Psychoanalyst, New Haven, CT

"If you're a Harry Potter fan, you are going to love this book! It is the most creative adventure story I have read in a long, long time. Even after I finished the book, I couldn't stop thinking about the characters and the story. It really makes you think."

—Hanna, age 11, grade 6

"Entertaining and intriguing! This book is so good you can't put it down. I finished it in one night! If you love adventures, you will love this book."

—Paige, age 11, Grade 6

"I'm kind of a science geek, and there's lots of really fun science in this book! Frankie travels through outer space in a space-time tunnel, to a planet with two moons and lavender humans who evolved by the ocean, so they can hold their breath underwater and "paddle" long distances with their webbed feet. I've never read a story like it. I felt like the author wrote it just for me."

—Logan, age 13, Grade 8

"When I was done with Frankie's adventure, I read the book all over again. I didn't want to let the story go. My favorite part was Frankie's daring climb down the chute on Krog Pad Island to save Iktae. I felt like I was right there with Frankie, and I get goosebumps every time I think about it! I read a lot of books, but this one really stood out. I'm recommending it to all my friends!"

—Eleanor, age 12, Grade 7

"This book is fun and exciting in every way. The anagrams were really creative, and I loved unscrambling them. I finally figured out that Krog Park stood for "dog park" and that made me laugh because the Krog Padders are so much like dogs, always playing and never thinking about the future. I will never look at the world the same way after reading *Frankie and the Gift of Fantasy*. I feel like I'm as changed as the characters were at the end of the story, when Frankie returned home."

—Clarice, age 11, Grade 6

Frankie and the Gift of Fantasy

TALES BY MOONS-LIGHT SERIES

Frankie

and the *Gift* of

Fantasy

RUTHY BALLARD

WHIPSMART
—— BOOKS ——
Science Through Stories

FRANKIE AND THE GIFT OF FANTASY
and the *Tales by Moons-light Series*
Copyright © 2021 by Ruth Ballard

Printed in the United States of America

Publisher's Cataloging-In-Publication Data
(Prepared by The Donohue Group, Inc.)

Names: Ballard, Ruthy, author.
Title: Frankie and the gift of fantasy / Ruthy Ballard.
Description: Sacramento, California : Whip Smart Books, [2020] |
    Series: Tales by moons-light series | Interest age level: 009-012. |
    Summary: "Frankie Russo doesn't brood about the past or worry
    about the future. He lives in the present moment, frolicking in a
    world of make-believe that drives his high-achieving parents crazy.
    They have lofty ambitions for him, but Frankie has no interest ...
    Frankie's parents nag him endlessly, worried he'll come to nothing.
    But all that changes when he disappears through a mysterious
    crack in his bedroom ceiling and finds himself on a distant, two-
    mooned planet called Urth"-- Provided by publisher.
Identifiers: ISBN 9780997853278 (paperback) | ISBN 9780997853285
    (Kindle) | ISBN 9780997853292 (ePub)
Subjects: LCSH: Boys--Outer space--Juvenile fiction. | Missing persons-
    -Juvenile fiction. | Imagination--Juvenile fiction. | Parent and
    child--Juvenile fiction. | CYAC: Boys--Outer space--Fiction. | Missing
    persons--Fiction. | Imagination--Fiction. | Parent and child--Fiction.
    | LCGFT: Science fiction. | Action and adventure fiction.
Classification: LCC PZ7.1.B35 Fr 2020 (print) | LCC PZ7.1.B35 (ebook) |
    DDC [Fic]--dc23

ISBN: 978-0-9978532-7-8 (paperback)
ISBN: 978-0-9978532-8-5 (Kindle)
ISBN: 978-0-9978532-9-2 (ePub)

Whipsmart Books
Sacramento, California

www.whipsmartbooks.com

To Sleeli, who has the gift of *Looking Closely*

"There is a crack in everything.
That's how the light gets in."

—LEONARD COHEN
Singer, Songwriter, Poet, Novelist

Contents

Acknowledgments

Publishing this book required the combined effort of a tribe of dedicated professionals, loving friends, and members of my family, to whom I'm forever grateful.

The members of the WhipSmart Books publishing team shepherded the project through its many phases. With publishing navigator Janica Smith and marketer Gail Kearns at the helm, the book was in good hands from the very start. Later, my editor, Jenny Bowman, provided expert guidance to make Frankie's story as strong and compelling as it could be, and my book designers, Alan Hebel and Ian Koviak, magically brought the cover and interior to life. Finally, Carmen Farmer, proofreader extraordinaire, added the finishing touches, drilling in deep to correct typos and other errors that escaped everyone's keen eyes but hers.

My dear friends Stephanie French, Angelica Kaner, and Leslie Lange, provided encouragement and feedback throughout the process, especially in the early days when the manuscript was rough and messy and needed loving, gentle hands.

Edie Ballard always had open ears and wonderful things to say (thanks, Mom!), and my children, Loren and Peter, helped, too. Loren offered invaluable comments about the astronomy, correcting many errors of fact (and teaching me much along the way!), while Peter served as my "go-to" expert about rock climbing. But most of all, my husband Ernie provided constructive criticism on more drafts than I can count, and created a safe, joyous life where my creativity could bloom.

I am also deeply indebted to the children in the WhipSmart Books' Early Reader Program, who helped me experience the book through young, fresh eyes. Many read Frankie's tale during the early days of the COVID-19 pandemic, and I'm grateful that they turned to the book for entertainment and adventure during those dark, uncertain times. For acknowledgment purposes, each chose a rename and identified their gift. Like Frankie, they are on magical journeys to authenticity, and I wish them wonder and good speed in their travels.

- Laura (Aural), Gift of *Caring for Others*, age 13, Oberlin, OH

- Wyatt (Yawtt), Gift of *Loving Dogs*, age 12, Edmonds, WA

- Michael (Hi Camel), Gift of *Drawing Cartoons*, age 9, San Jose, CA
- Kate (Take), Gift of *Dreaming Big Dreams*, age 10, Los Angeles, California
- Nasikare (Air Snake), Gift of *Thinking for Herself*, age 13, Chicago, IL
- Eliza Jane (Lizea Jena), Gift of *Creativity*, age 11, Oberlin, OH
- Arsenio (Iron Sea), Gift of *Reading*, age 9, Los Angeles, CA
- Nate (Neat), Gift of *Cooking*, age 10, Reno, NV
- Melody Ann (Many Led On), Gift of *Playing Piano*, age 13, Jacksonville, FL
- Barron (Ron Bar), Gift of *Building*, age 7, Falls Church, VA
- Amy (Mya), Gift of *Fashion*, age 12, Sacramento, CA
- Christopher (Chip Shorter), Gift of *Playing Soccer*, age 10, Sacramento, CA
- Joshua James (Jamahue Joss), age 8, Gift of *Making Stuff Work*, Detroit, MI
- Eleanor (Real One), age 13, Gift of *Many Feelings*, Rancho Cordova, CA
- Lorien (Norlie), age 11, Gift of *Creativity*, Lincoln, NE
- Kinley (Nikley), age 10, Gift of *Dancing*, Lincoln, NE
- Clarice (A Circle), age 11, Gift of *Happiness*, Houston, TX

The Crack

Frankie Russo was lucky in many ways. Unlike another boy with the same name, who lived in a hut in a distant country with two crotchety great-aunts and four goats, Frankie lived in a fine house by the sea in Monterey, California.

The Russo house was not a hut. Far from it. With five bedrooms, a cozy family room full of books and pictures, and an enormous sunny kitchen, it was quite a palace. What's more, Frankie didn't share this cushy abode with great-aunts and goats. Instead, he lived with two well-to-do parents, his younger brother Alex, and a good-natured dog named Mush.

Frankie had plenty to eat, too, which the Frankie with the aunts and goats did not, and he fueled his naturally athletic body at every opportunity. In fact, he could have kicked a soccer ball harder and farther than any of his friends, if he'd wanted to.

But Frankie wasn't like the other boys at Hatfield Elementary. Nor was he like his hard-driven "helicopter parents," who had lofty ambitions for him. Instead, he preferred to do nothing, or what appeared to be nothing to his parents, but was actually very exciting. You see, Frankie had the delightful gift of *Fantasy*, a rare talent for spinning up fun, improbable stories in his mind. His parents should have been enchanted, but that's where his luck ran out. They viewed him as purposely, unforgivably lazy instead, and gave him a terrible time.

"Run for the ball, Frankie! Stop standing out there with your head in the clouds!" his father, Roberto, would yell at soccer practice, hoping his son would "hop to."

But Frankie didn't "hop to." Instead, he stayed right where he was, lost in a wonderful daydream: playing hyper-soccer on the moon, where balls soared several miles and the members of the opposing team were transparent snakes with wings.

"You'll never amount to anything," Roberto often scolded. "You have so much *potential*, Frankie, but you're wasting it."

His mother, Evelyn, was equally concerned, but she tended to cajole, not yell. "Come on, honey, I know you can solve this math problem. Just apply yourself a little harder. Stop fiddling with your pencil. It's not a sword."

Frankie wondered how his mother could be so

blind. Of *course* his pencil was a sword. And if she'd just leave him alone, he'd have plenty of fun with it, too, slaying a purple, fire-breathing dragon in the mountains of Venus.

"What are we going to do about him?" his parents constantly asked each other. "How can we get him motivated to succeed? He'll never go to college. When he's all grown up, he won't be able to get a job. Alex will be a doctor, lawyer, or engineer one day, but Frankie will be lying in a gutter."

Frankie sometimes overhead these verbal exchanges, and, though they hurt his feelings, he tried to shrug them off. He didn't want to go to college, nor get one of the three "acceptable" adult jobs they had in mind. Not when he could flip helium burgers on Jupiter or rule a kingdom of mermen in the Caspian Sea, up inside his head, where all the fun was.

Rebukes like "Feed Mush. It's your only chore!" or "Finish your homework, or you'll be grounded for a week!" fell on deaf ears. Frankie had stopped listening a long time ago. "BLAH, BLAH, BLAH" was all he ever heard. His parents always stepped in to pull in the slack. When he forgot to feed Mush, they did it for him. When he dawdled over his homework, they finished it on his behalf, worried he'd fail out of school. Thus, Frankie was free to spend his time in more interesting ventures, like saving Earth from a Martian invasion or cycling to the moon on his BMX bike. If only if his parents had stopped pushing and nagging, he'd have been quite content. As it was, he slunk around most of the time, just out of reach, fearful his parents would pounce at any time.

"I wish he'd come with an owner's manual," his mother sighed one Saturday afternoon, a few weeks after Frankie's tenth birthday. "Instead, he came wrapped in a blue blanket with an encouraging smile from a nurse. Our coffee grinder came with more instructions!"

Frankie's father grunted his agreement. He was on his way out the door to the bank. "Lucky we don't have anything scheduled for Frankie today. I'm tired out with trying to make him cooperate."

Evelyn was an amateur photographer with work to do, so she disappeared into the family room with her camera and laptop. Alex, meanwhile, walked to the Just Hangin' Out Rock Gym to climb with friends. Frankie, on the other hand, was upstairs in his bedroom doing (you guessed it) what appeared to be nothing. In point-of-fact, he was very busy, lying on his bed, staring at the ceiling, daydreaming that he lived on a star.

"I'd have to wear a fireproof suit, of course," he thought, "or I'd burn up." And it was just then, as he was fashioning the special-order Kevlar suit in his mind, that he first saw *the crack*.

Many people wouldn't have noticed the crack, for it was quite ordinary. But children like Frankie spend many hours staring at their bedroom ceilings because they're so often sent to their rooms as punishment.

Thus, they're intimately familiar with their bedroom ceilings and notice when something is amiss.

The crack was *new*, of that he was sure, and he found himself strangely drawn to it.

He thought, "If I stand on my bed and stretch all the way up, I might be able to touch it."

He couldn't quite manage it. Even with the help of his rarely used desk chair (which wobbled uncertainly on the mattress as he tried to climb it), the crack was tantalizingly out of reach. He tried to jump the last few inches, and his right forefinger almost breached the distance, but the chair twisted sideways and sent him crashing to the floor.

He bumped his head, but he didn't notice because his finger commanded his full attention. It was tingling fiercely, and, as he watched in amazement, it turned a magnificent shade of purple that reminded him of the Lush Lavender crayon in his Kidz Art Craft Set.

The Frankie who lived in the hut with the great aunts and goats would have thrown a spear at the crack. At the age of twelve, he was the head of his little family, and it was his job to protect the others. But the Frankie in Monterey took his safety for granted. He lived in a fine house by the sea, not in a hut in the middle of lion country. He had no spears, except in his imagination, where, of course, he had a castle full of them.

The tingling sensation dissipated quickly, but the lavender color lingered, and, after a few minutes, Frankie grew alarmed. If he arrived at dinner with a purple finger, his parents would accuse him of goofing off all day instead of doing something productive, like retirement planning. He didn't want another "BLAH, BLAH, BLAH" lecture.

In the hope of a speedy solution, he took off for the kitchen.

As Frankie passed the stove on the way to the sink, he suddenly realized he was starving. Not starving in the way that his namesake with the goats and aunts sometimes starved (going to bed hungry four nights a week), but starving in a way that a well-fed boy thinks he's hungry whenever he smells food. A pot of spaghetti sauce was simmering in a large pot, and its aroma filled the air. Thus, he forgot about his finger for a few minutes, and, using a nearby wooden spoon, finished off about half of it.

When he was done, he walked over to the sink and squeezed a healthy dose of liquid dish soap on his finger. He used a scrub brush as an aid, but nothing happened. What now? He needed a way out of his dilemma.

"I'll tell mom that Alex painted my finger while I was sleeping," Frankie thought. "That will get *me* off the hook and *him* into trouble!"

Frankie wasn't a mean kid, but Alex annoyed him. His parents were always saying things like, "Look at Alex! He doesn't muck around! Watch him monkey up the wall at the rock gym, earning the top prize. Watch him whiz through his homework. BLAH, BLAH, BLAH."

These comparisons made Frankie feel very small, and he often indulged in revenge fantasies: Alex failing out of second grade, Alex booted off the baseball team, *Alex in jail.*

Fortunately (at least for Alex), Frankie didn't have to lie. He discovered that soda did the trick. When he poured Garth's Wild West Root Beer over his finger and scrubbed it in, the stubborn stain gradually came off and slithered down the drain.

Having achieved his aim, Frankie was eager to get back to his room. The crack seemed to be calling out to him, and, if the purple color reappeared, he'd know what to do. Thus, after a brief interruption to answer the front door, he made his way back to his bed, grabbing a well-used desk chair from Alex's room along the way. He needed two desk chairs for the task he had in mind, and when he placed them atop one other, he felt certain that if he scrambled up, he'd be able to explore the longed-for crack just fine.

It was a difficult maneuver. The pile of wood and boy collapsed three times before Frankie was successful. But on the fourth attempt, his makeshift, wobbly apparatus held, and he reached up, thrilled to finally capture his prize. He sensed, somehow, that the crack offered a way out of the Academic Awards Ceremony at Hatfield Elementary the next day, where every kid would be getting a plaque, except him. He was dreading the ceremony and the "BLAH, BLAH, BLAH" lecture that would follow. He hoped that when he touched the crack something wonderful would happen, and his problem at school would evaporate.

He was not disappointed.

ZING!

The moment the tip of his finger met the crack, a jolt of electricity shot from his finger through his body and out his toes before the room disappeared from view and he was somewhere else altogether.

If you'd been in the room with Frankie and blinked your eyes at the wrong time, you'd have missed seeing him vanish.

I would be remiss to lead you into the next few hours of Frankie's unusual day without advising you to bring along some peanut butter sandwiches and a sword, for Frankie had neither and would soon regret it. But you've been forewarned and can run off and get them now. Then perhaps you'll be willing to share them with Frankie when we all get to where we're going, in Chapter Two.

2

What Happened Next

First, let me apologize about the sword. It was a teaser. Frankie is not going to need one, so you can return it to your sword closet, with all your others. Writers sometimes get a little ahead of themselves, especially at the end of the first chapter of an exciting book.

The peanut butter sandwiches, however, are another story. Frankie will be desperate for them soon, and whether or not he gets them will require an important decision on your part. So, hold onto them for now. If you like, you can draw them on a piece of paper and tuck the sketch away in your pirate's treasure box (if you're lucky enough to have one). Then, when you need the sandwiches, you can pull the drawing out, ready to go.

Now, let's return to Frankie.

The moment the violent jolt of electricity exited his toes, the crack opened up and he shot through it. Then it snapped shut, returning to its original, ordinary appearance, as if nothing had happened.

For one brief (but creepy) moment, Frankie found himself crouching in the cramped crawl space between his bedroom ceiling and the roof, staring into the eyes of a resident rat. But it was a short-lived encounter, for a mysterious force sucked him upward so fast that his body thinned and distorted into a long, flexible noodle, slender enough to thread through a small hole in the roof and into the blue sky beyond.

Up, up, up he went, soaring through layer after layer of Earth's atmosphere, the sky growing darker and darker with each passing second until it was blacker than black and exploding with millions of twinkling stars. It was an astounding sight but didn't last long, for the stars quickly changed shape, morphing into colorful streaks. By then, you see, Frankie was shooting faster than the speed of light through a space-time tunnel on his way to a distant planet called Urth. And when you're in a space-time tunnel, stars look pretty weird.

It was fortunate that his trip was speedy, for outer space is a hostile place for a human, and it's best to cross it as quickly as possible. Frankie soon found himself gasping for breath and chilled to the bone, for the vast empty space between stars is airless and bitterly cold. But worst of all, the sudden change in external air pressure forced the gases in his lungs to expand and the water in his soft tissues to vaporize. The sensation was bizarre and so painful that Frankie instinctively tried to close his eyes, to block out what was happening. But to his alarm, his lids wouldn't budge. The vacuum of space was tugging on his eyeballs, sucking them forward. Closing his eyes was impossible, and he was in danger of losing them altogether.

No one wants to die as a blind, bubbling ice cube gasping for air, so I'm pleased to inform you that Frankie was spared this fate. Instead, the worst he suffered was a nasty sunburn from exposure to ultraviolet light as he whizzed past Urth's sun, and he arrived at his final destination unscathed and back to his normal human-boy shape again, standing upright in the middle of an alien forest, surrounded by trees bearing round, purple fruit.

The forest was eerily quiet, and, after his adventure through space, Frankie instinctively knew he was no longer on Earth. But while you and I might have been a little nervous, and maybe even scuffled our feet to make some noise to keep us company, Frankie stood still for more than a minute, feeling, more than anything else, that he'd arrived *home*. If you've ever come back from a long vacation, even one that was lots of fun, and felt an overwhelming sense of peace when you walked in your front door, you'll know how it was for Frankie. He'd never felt safer and happier in his entire life.

Frankie tried to hold onto the feeling, but it slipped away, and soon he was examining himself to make sure he wasn't injured. He seemed okay; no bones were broken. But all eight of his fingertips were purple now—an even brighter shade than before, mirroring the Psychedelic Grape crayon he liked to use when drawing space creatures in the margins of his history textbook.

Frankie wasn't concerned, though. He figured he wouldn't be seeing his parents for a while, so who cared about Psychedelic Grape fingers? Thus, instead of running off and hunting through the unfamiliar forest for soda, he walked over to the nearest tree and climbed into its dark branches, wondering if the purple fruit tasted sweet and juicy, like oranges, or bitter and chewy, like the curly mustard greens his mother so often served for dinner.

As it turned out, it tasted like a bad version of stale bread. It was so awful that he spit out the slimy mess immediately and even then, his mouth went dry and his tongue stuck to the roof of his mouth, his lips in a pucker.

"Yuk!" he thought. "I won't be eating any more of *that*!"

Trying to decide what to do next, Frankie noticed that the network of branches that surrounded him looked an awful lot like a jungle gym. The branches were smooth and just the right distance apart to swing from one to the next. Thus, he turned his attention to playing King of the Purple Fruit Monkeys for a while, making his way through the forest, arm over arm, warding off other monkeys who dared encroach upon his territory. Purple Fruit Monkeys, it turned out, fought a great deal, but Frankie let them know who was boss.

The Frankie who lived in the hut overseas would have climbed high in the forest canopy to get a bird's-eye view of his surroundings. There were plenty of *real* monkeys in his part of the world, and he'd been taught to avoid them because they carried disease. But "Monterey Frankie" had acrophobia (a strong, irrational fear of high places) and had no idea that monkeys could be dangerous. Instead, he played King of the Purple Fruit Monkeys in perfect health, close to the ground for the next four hours, which I shall skip over to save time, and it was nearly sunset before it dawned on him that dinnertime was fast approaching, and he'd have to eat the yucky purple fruit again or waste away.

It didn't occur to Frankie that he might fix his own dinner, by scouting through the forest to find something edible and then cooking it up over a makeshift camp fire. The Frankie with the aunts and goats, when faced with such a situation, would have known exactly what to do.

But our Frankie didn't know how to light a fire by rubbing two sticks together. Nor could he tell the difference between foods that were likely to be edible and those that were poisonous. Dinners at the fine house by the sea appeared on the table as if by magic, delivered by his parents, piping hot, from a fancy induction stove they'd imported from Europe. And his mother, who did most of the grocery shopping, bought everything from the Monterey Food Co-op. She didn't train Frankie to forage because she had no idea how to do it herself.

In truth, Frankie was nowhere close to starvation. He had a good two weeks of wiggle room before things could get out of hand. However, since he'd never missed a meal, he didn't know what real hunger was like, so he felt sorry for himself, spinning a story that a forest that had felt so wonderfully homey at first had unfairly betrayed him by failing to provide dinner at the expected hour.

You can decide at this point whether you want to give Frankie the peanut butter sandwiches you brought with you into this chapter. But I advise against it, because someone else in this story will soon need them much more than well-fed Frankie, and you may wish to give them to her instead.

Convinced he wouldn't last the night (unless you gave him the sandwiches), Frankie sat on a branch, his bare legs hanging into empty space, and watched the sun go down. He didn't actually see it set, of course, as he hadn't clambered up the trees to get a proper view. If he had, he would have enjoyed a beautiful sight as the sun disappeared into a glorious tropical ocean, shaded by puffy clouds tinged with gold. But he knew it was setting because the sky mellowed to a soft blue-grey, followed by a midnight blue, and stars flickered to life where the once-bright sky had been.

Soon, Frankie could see dozens of stars, shining like the fires of a distantly encamped army, spread at uneven distances among unseen hills and valleys. It was a vast army, he decided, one that carried horse-loads of delicious food. He imagined himself as an abducted prince. The army had been searching for him for weeks. When they found him, they'd carry him back to the palace and set a huge feast before him, including pancakes slathered with butter and hot chocolate with a dash of cinnamon, just the way he liked it.

Frankie didn't know the names of the constellations at home. He couldn't point out anything but the Big Dipper on a good night. Thus, he had no clue that the patterns of the stars above him were completely new. What he did notice, however, and with some confusion, was that as soon as the sky was quite dark, it started to get light again, as if the sun was coming back up after merely dipping below the horizon.

An eerie kind of twilight gradually took the stars away as he sat among the purple fruit, staring at the sky and fantasizing about food. The constellation that had looked like a pile of steaming spaghetti topped with a healthy dose of grated Romano cheese, blinked out. The circle of stars shaped like a gooey pizza faded away. And in the east... well, what was in the east requires its own paragraph to describe.

Not even "starving" Frankie could imagine that what was rising above the trees in the east looked anything like food. At first, he thought he was having double vision, and he closed his eyes for a moment to clear them. But when he reopened them, the apparition was still there: two full moons peeking through the tangled branches of the trees. The first was very large, at least twice the size of Earth's moon, and much brighter. The second was about the size of Earth's moon, but dimmer, and pale orange.

Perhaps you've had the profoundly uneasy feeling that Frankie experienced as he sat, awestruck, watching the moons make their grand entrance. His overwhelming urge was to hide—like a panicked mouse in the shade of a hawk's wing—and he threw his arms around the nearest tree branch and burrowed his head into it. But the brightness of the moons-light (for *moons*-light it was) penetrated through his tightly puckered eyelids, and even Frankie, with his well-developed skill for disappearing into his head, could not escape.

Quick as lightning, he slid down the tree and fled as fast as he could, away from the moons and the terrifying moons-light, his moons-shadow leaping before him as he ran.

The moons-light was so bright that he had no trouble seeing where he was going, and his natural athleticism served him well. Hurdling over tree roots and downed branches like an Olympic track star, mouth wide open with fright, he flew across the forest until he reached

Frankie fled as fast as he could...

a meadow surrounded by granite boulders the size of houses. It was there, in the searing light of the two moons, that he spied a cave, and, at the same instant, used his best soccer goalie moves to dive through the opening.

Frankie's heart beat wildly. His mouth went bone

dry. As he slid, he skinned his hands, and they throbbed with pain. For the first time that day, despite the delightful feeling he'd experienced when he'd first arrived, all he wanted to do was go home. Alone (or so he thought), he crawled to the back of the cave, as far from the scary moons-light as he could possibly get.

Bringing his knees to his chest, he huddled in a defensive posture, keeping one eye on the mouth of the cave lest the moons swoop down from the heavens, crawl through the opening, and gobble him up. It was two or three minutes before he realized that this event was unlikely, and he felt safe enough to let down his guard.

The entrance to the cave was very small, but, inside, it was large enough for a person to stand up and move about. Moons-light poured through the opening, but Frankie sensed, now, that he'd overreacted. Moons didn't attack people, no matter how fierce they might seem. Back home, on Earth, the moon sometimes looked enormous, especially when it was near the horizon, but it didn't leap down from the heavens and hunt people down.

"Besides," he thought, "after my trip through outer space, I'm obviously on a distant planet, and other worlds might have multiple moons. Why not? Saturn has a bunch, I think."

Frankie was right (at last count, Saturn has sixty-two) and his unease drained away. Suddenly, the whole idea of running away from moons seemed overblown, and he stood up, a little shakily, to find out where he was.

3

Where Frankie Was

Where Frankie was is best described from the perspective of the other occupant of the cave, an alien woman named Ideth, whom he'll be meeting soon. She had webbed feet, purple skin, and a layer of indigo blubber around her torso, and her duty was to find a child.

If you live in a place where parents keep close eyes on their offspring, rarely letting them wander about on their own, you probably find this odd. Why did Ideth need to *find* a child? What kind of parent would let their kid go missing? But Urth is a different planet with its own traditions, and Ideth had never met the child she was seeking. The child would be a traveler from the other side of the galaxy, on loan to her for a while. And since she'd never met the child before, she couldn't very well keep tabs on him, or her, as the case might be. At least not yet.

"Findlings" (as they were called) were different from traditional children in other ways, too. They didn't arrive on Urth as howling infants that looked like wrinkly old men and burped up milk a lot. Moreover, Ideth's task wasn't to raise them to adults who, in turn, would raise howling, wrinkled infants of their own. Instead, her sole duty was to take her findlings under her protection and guide them to the right place at the right time without losing them along the way. It was an important job requiring extensive training to do well, and she was proud that none of her children thus far had come to harm (though once, she had to admit, one had come perilously close).

To master the needed skills, Ideth had attended an elite school called an Uppy Academy, where she'd "striped" in a gift, which is similar to majoring in a subject in college. She'd hemmed and hawed a bit at first, taking several months to choose her destiny. But she'd finally settled on *Fantasy*, because her academic advisor told her that it would be an excellent complement to her own gift of *Reading Minds*.

He said, "Just think of all the fun you'll have. What's the point of eavesdropping on the thoughts of a child with the gift of *Worrying* or the gift of *Liking Spiders*? That would be a bummer, wouldn't it?"

Once she'd chosen her stripe, Ideth's professional fate was sealed, for her stripe governed what kind of child she'd be permitted to find after she'd earned her degree. A graduate who striped in *Forging New Paths*, for example, would be eligible to find a child with that exciting gift. But she couldn't find a child with the gift of *Enjoying Astrophysics*. That interesting, rather complicated child would belong to another.

Ideth had found thirty-two findlings with the gift of *Fantasy* thus far and guided them successfully, but her last two attempts had been disappointing. Sometimes, children failed to appear, and she'd gone home to Cairntip Island, several hundred miles away, empty-handed. This time, she hoped to have better luck.

A few weeks earlier, Ideth, and several others like her, called uppies, had traveled to Finding Island, a tiny dot in Urth's Eastern Sea, thick with Finding Trees bearing tasteless, pucker-inducing purple Finding Fruit. There, she'd separated herself from the group, as was the custom, and wandered about, looking for a cave where she could hunker down and wait. Findlings didn't arrive on a strict schedule; it could be days, weeks, or months before they appeared. And there were no comfy hotels on Finding Island. It was completely undeveloped. Thus, choosing a suitable cave was vital if one wanted to enjoy time camping out. Some uppies preferred to sleep outside in the open, but Ideth had been caught in a storm once, and had switched to caves long ago.

Several earlier caves had proved damp and uncomfortable. One had even given Ideth a nasty rash. Finally, she'd found one she liked, and she'd set up camp along one end, using a conveniently located fissure to serve as a smoke hole for her cooking fire. It was there that she'd spent her days living off the nasty Finding Fruit, and her nights dreaming of children.

The months passed. Urth's two moons, Lunera and Ru, cycled through their phases, and Ideth grew tired of the Finding Fruit. It was the only food she was permitted to eat on a finding, and though it was much better cooked than raw, there were only a dozen or so recipes to prepare the stuff. The fruit was nutritious and popular in health food stores on busy, bustling Cairntip. Myth had it that Finding Fruit cured all kinds of ills. But for uppies, who had to subsist on it for long periods, its purple flesh held no allure. She'd begged and prayed to the heavens for her findling to appear, if only to break the tasteless tedium she was enduring. Yet day after day had passed with no findling and no end of the Finding Fruit. Soon, she'd have to admit defeat and return to Cairntip once more.

If you saved the peanut butter sandwiches, now is the time to valiantly whip them out and give them to Ideth. They are a forbidden treat, but if she finds them magically waiting for her on her pillow, she will wolf them down, I can assure you.

Hungry or not, Ideth pulled the covers over her head, alone and depressed, and eventually fell asleep. She dreamt of a boy with bright red hair, whose gift was *Heroism*. In prior dreams, the child had been a Japanese boy with a wicked smile who had the gift

of *Humor*; a freckled-faced girl with soft blue eyes
who *Loved Animals*; a heavy-set boy from Zanzibar
who *Slept Soundly*. Each child, in turn, had marched
through her nightly visions but then disappeared, for
they were not hers. As Ideth slept, the red-haired boy
did a dream-dance, recklessly stomping over her frontal
cortex (heroic children can sometimes be a bit destruc-
tive), and she tossed and turned. But she would have
sat bolt upright had she known that her findling was
running headlong through the Finding Forest toward
her at that very moment, seconds away from making his
noisy entrance.

CLUMP! CRASH! CRASH! echoed off the cave walls.

"Ouch!" Frankie cried, as he skidded to a stop.

Ideth woke with a start. She opened her eyes and let
out an involuntary gasp. In the past, her findlings had
arrived quietly. She'd heard stories of sudden arrivals,
but not one as jolting as this. Her eyes followed the child
as he fled to the far wall and curled into a fetal position.
She wondered if he was real.

"Am I still asleep?" she asked herself. "Perhaps this
is a nightmare sent to test my patience and forbearance,
sent to torture me for one more night with the promise
of a findling."

In other, less dramatic circumstances, Ideth would
have gone to him immediately. Instead, unsure if the
boy was what he seemed, she hesitated. She wanted,
fiercely, for the child to be hers, and she was afraid of

the crushing disappointment that would follow if he were just a dream.

Soon, though, Ideth's training from the Uppy Academy kicked in, and she made her move. When the child stood up, and she could see him properly, she crossed over to him.

And oh! He was so clearly an Earth child, solidly built, with lean muscles and flawless skin, and just the right age for a findling. But his real beauty was in his big brown eyes, which shone, unblinking, like two steady lanterns.

There was no more confusion then. The eyes told her. Her child, a boy with the gift of *Fantasy*, had arrived. Such children always had eyes that seemed lit from within. And he'd appeared at the most auspicious time for a finding, too—at a harvest syzygy, when both moons were full, the night skies were almost as bright as day, the ocean pulled far away from the land at low tide, and there were shellfish and crabs for the taking.

It seemed too good to be true but there was no doubt, no doubt at all.

So, when the boy looked directly at her and asked in a whisper, "Who are you?" she felt no further hesitation.

"I'm Ideth," she replied. "I'm your uppy."

4

What's Been Happening in Monterey

T here is *nothing* more painful for a parent than losing a child. Imagine that you have a favorite pet (and if you do, this mental exercise will be easier) and one day it simply disappears. If it's a dog, perhaps you left him in the yard, and when you come home, he's no longer there. Or if it's a goldfish, you walk into the living room and find her fishbowl empty. In addition to the profound feeling of loss, you would also feel responsible, because caring for the pet was your job and you failed to protect it. There's also the *not knowing what happened*, which can be almost as bad because, over time, it can eat you alive inside.

At first, Frankie's parents were annoyed when he didn't show up for dinner.

"Where is he?" Evelyn asked, staring at his empty seat. "Has he arranged to eat dinner at a friend's house? Maybe he's goofing around and lost track of time."

Then they got angry.

"What the heck is he doing?" Roberto frowned. "What game is he playing? How can he do this to us?"

But as time passed, their anger slowly turned to concern, their concern turned to fear, and their fear turned into the worst feeling of all: terror.

They called the parents of all his friends. They went through their fine house checking under every bed, in every bathtub, in every closet. They went out into the yard and called his name. They peered fearfully into their swimming pool and walked up and down the block screaming, "Frankie! Frankie!" Finally, they called the police. By nine that evening, a police helicopter was in the air scanning the neighborhood and nearby beaches with a bright spotlight. By eleven o'clock, the television news crews had arrived.

Evelyn clutched her cell phone, afraid to put it down in case Frankie called. Roberto spoke to the news crews and gave them a recent photo of Frankie for broadcast. Alex was so terrified that he refused to leave his mother's side.

As the hours passed, the house filled with police officers and crime scene investigators, who questioned everyone and took Frankie's toothbrush for DNA.

"If his body is ever found," a cop named Joshua

Morgan explained unfeelingly, "the DNA on his tooth-brush will allow us to identify him. DNA is very helpful in such instances."

Evelyn's heart dropped and Roberto's hair stood on end. *If his body is ever found?* Did the cops think that Frankie was dead?

The police went through the Russo's fine house from top to bottom, and gathered photos off Evelyn's computer: Frankie playing soccer. Frankie at a friend's birthday party eating pizza. Frankie grinning with friends at summer camp. Frankie fiddling with a pencil. They interviewed his parents repeatedly.

When did you last see him? What was he wearing? Was he upset about anything? Who are his friends and where do they live? Has he ever disappeared like this before?

To each question, his family gave their best answers.

"I was the one who saw him last," Evelyn said, choking down tears. "I sent him to his bedroom for dawdling over his homework. He was wearing a pair of black shorts and a red t-shirt. He had socks on, I think, but no shoes."

"He's a daydreamer," Roberto added. "He often misses deadlines. But he never misses meals. Here's a list of the kids he sometimes hangs out with in the neighbor-hood. And no, no, no—he has never disappeared like this before."

Most missing children, the police assured them, were found within twenty-four hours of their disappearance.

So, as friends and family members began arriving in Monterey the next morning, eager to help, they all offered comforting words.

"Don't worry, he'll show up soon. They're bound to find him. The police are trained for this kind of thing. They know what they're doing."

Frankie's grandmother even said, "Goodness, we'll all be laughing about this by the same time tomorrow," which was received very coldly, but excused because she was elderly and "not quite all there" (if you know what I mean).

Alex was especially hard hit. He was a gregarious but sensitive child, and the sudden loss of his brother left him heartsick. But he wasn't the kind of person to remain paralyzed by fear for long. He had the gift of *Getting Things Done,* and doers desperately need to be busy, so his mind raced this way and that trying to think of a way he could help.

"We need to put up flyers!" he shouted suddenly. "That's what they do on TV when a kid is missing!"

Alex fled to his bedroom to make one. His flyer wasn't perfect, and Evelyn (who had the gift of *Perfectionism*) found a couple of spelling errors and corrected them. Otherwise, the flyer looked great. Evelyn made hundreds of copies, and a few hours later, dozens of people were scattering to different areas of Monterey and nearby towns with masking tape and pushpins in hand.

People scattered to put up the posters, pushpins in hand...

"MISSING BOY" was emblazoned across the top of the flyer, followed by Alex's description of his brother and a photograph of Frankie in his soccer uniform. There was also the promise of a $50,000 reward. Frankie's father phoned his investment adviser and instructed him to sell off some of their stock. He was sure that by the time someone called with a lead, which he desperately prayed would be soon, he'd be able to pony up the cash. He had to.

The fact that Evelyn had taken literally thousands of photographs of her ne'er-do-well son was a definite plus. She saturated the media with photographs of Frankie that morning, and Channel 12 broadcast a very impressive photo of him head-butting a soccer ball. His disappearance was the leading story by noon.

The head of the Missing Children's Task Force, an organization that assisted families in the early stages of a possible abduction case, stopped by mid-afternoon. Two well-meaning, businesslike women came to the house to advise Frankie's parents about setting up a volunteer center to coordinate a search independent of the police investigation.

One of them turned a pair of pitying eyes on Evelyn and said, "You know, dear, the police are screw ups. Why, our David has been missing for more than two years, and they haven't turned up a single lead."

This wasn't what Evelyn had hoped to hear, of course, but at least the women were going to help them find Frankie, and for that she was grateful.

There were also calls from two psychics. The first provided a vague description of Frankie's location as "near a lake or large body of water, with some kind of greenery, and perhaps a culvert." She whipped off an email that detailed her retainer agreement: "$10,000. Non-refundable."

"Ten thousand dollars!" Evelyn groaned. "She's a thief!"

The second psychic offered up her services "free to grieving souls" and then delivered the crushing blow: "He's dead, poor thing. But I guess you already suspected that."

Frankie's parents were exhausted but unable to sleep. A friend led Evelyn to a back bedroom and made her lie down, "even if it's just for a few minutes, honey."

But it was no use. Even as Evelyn's eyes closed, her heart hammered, her stomach cramped, and her mind raced from one scenario to another, searching desperately for hope in any corner where it might be hiding.

"Oh, please, please, *PLEASE*," she gasped, squeezing her eyes shut and rolling into a fetal position, a pillow between her knees. "Let him show up!"

Alex brought her a cup of tea, but she couldn't drink it.

As more hours passed with no news, the volunteers returned to their own homes for dinner, and the fine house by the sea became quiet. Frankie's parents crawled into bed beside one another, Alex between them, lost in an agony that only they could truly understand. Evelyn looked at the clock on the nightstand. It was 8:55 p.m.

"Oh, no," she whispered to Roberto with overwhelming dread. "It's been more than twenty-four hours."

There was a shuffle from the doorway as Frankie's grandmother made her way back to bed after a trip to the bathroom. "You know," she said with a little chuckle, popping her head into the bedroom, "we'll all be laughing about this the same time next week!"

Then she hobbled on down the hallway, thinking she'd said something helpful and uplifting when, in fact, her words hung like doom in the air.

5

Uppy Surfing
and Ducky Sacks

When someone goes missing, especially if that person is having an exciting adventure on the other side of the galaxy, it is much, *much* better to be the one missing than the ones left behind. In truth, Frankie hadn't given a moment's thought to what might be happening back home in Monterey.

Who can blame him? He'd been sucked through a crack in his bedroom ceiling, survived a journey of 64,000 light years through the vacuum of outer space, landed on a distant two-mooned planet, and met Ideth, his uppy, a rather odd-looking woman who seemed delighted to have "found" him.

"Urth is a long way from your planet," she explained. "If you drove your parents' car at seventy miles an hour all day and all night, it would take you six hundred billion years to get here. The space-time tunnel allows swift travel instead."

"How does it work?" Frankie asked.

"Oh, it's quite mysterious," she replied. "But I won't call it magic because the things we call magic often don't turn out to be magic, but simply things we don't understand yet. And when we understand them, we no longer call them magic."

Ideth was only an inch or two taller than Frankie and had the wrinkles and demeanor of his grandmother. She could be as old as sixty he guessed, though he was a very poor judge of age and might have been twenty years off either way. She puttered about like his grand-mother, too, a pair of glasses perched on her head and another hanging around her neck by a chain. She was kind, but Frankie had a hard time not staring at her Lush Lavender skin and webbed feet as she moved about. He had to admit, though, that he liked her one-piece swim-suit. It shimmered in the light of her hurricane lantern as she moved, reflecting different colors depending on the angle. He'd never seen a swimsuit like it.

"You see, Frankie," Ideth said, "we won't be staying on Finding Island for much longer. You belong on Krog Pad Island and it will be such a relief to get moving. I don't think I can stand one more day of Finding Fruit. I can almost taste the Krog Pad bluff berries and the win-nin nuts. It's the peak of the season for them."

"Why do I belong on Krog Pad?" Frankie asked.

"Because that's where you'll complete your mission," she said. "I have no clue what your mission is—we uppies never know—but it's an important one. You can bet on it.'"

Frankie momentarily hoped that his mission would involve a monster of some kind and that he'd chop off its three green heads to save the world. But he let the fantasy go and focused on Ideth instead. He loved the way she hovered about him, as if he were a prince. She paid rapt attention to everything he said. It was the first time Frankie had been the center of attention in a good way, and he opened right up.

"Sometimes I toss my homework in the dumpster by the school library on my way home," he chuckled, and she laughed right along.

For her part, Ideth was delighted. After her two recent failures, she'd finally found another child, and she was eager to get him where he needed to be. Her plan was to take Frankie to Krog Pad Island as soon as she'd sent up her flare the next morning. Laup, the boatman, would be watching for it and would bring them supplies for their paddle, including delicious foods she hadn't tasted in weeks.

Meanwhile, Frankie was wondering if Ideth, in her fancy swimsuit, was a triathlete. He was impressed at the thought that he might have landed among a race of super-athletes who could do a host of amazing things.

Hey! Maybe they could train *him* to be a super-athlete too, and, when he got back to Monterey, he'd go to the Olympics. His parents would forget all about Alex. They'd brag about *him* to their friends for once. He could see himself, on the Olympic podium, with ten gold medals hanging around his neck, waving to the crowd and the TV cameras. Reporters would hound him with questions. He'd be all over the news. When he got back to school, his classmates would whisper in the halls when he passed: "That's Frankie Russo, the guy who won ten Olympic gold medals in uppy surfing. No one's ever done that before!"

Frankie smiled as his fantasy came to its lofty end. When he opened his eyes (for he'd closed them to help himself imagine), he saw that Ideth was smiling too.

"That was a wonderful daydream, Frankie!" She clapped her hands, clearly charmed. "There's no such sport as uppy surfing, but the idea is delightful. Maybe we should invent it while you're here so you can earn your medals. Am I right, or am I right?"

Frankie's chest swelled with pleasure, but then he grew alarmed.

"How did you know about my fantasy?" he asked, a little off balance. He wasn't sure he liked the idea of someone eavesdropping on his imagination, which had always been his and his alone. But, at the same time, he was proud. In Monterey, he spent most of his "study hour" (which typically expanded into three or four hours of evading his parents' frustrated glares, exasperated sighs, and "helpful" suggestions) galloping through acres of unexplored dreamland, only to pay for it later ("BLAH, BLAH, BLAH"). Yet Ideth seemed entranced by his fantasies, and even egged him on.

"Oh, you won't have any secrets from me while you're here," she informed him. "I have the gift of *Reading Minds*. I'm quite skilled at it."

Frankie didn't know what to think. He knew that some people back on Earth claimed they could read minds, but he'd always figured they were faking.

Ideth continued. "Anyway, right now, I need to feed you and prepare a comfy place for you to sleep. I brought enough supplies for two, of course, hoping a findling would show up. And you're quite hungry and tired now. You must be."

Frankie suddenly felt exhausted, almost as if Ideth's words had put a spell on him. Being reminded of food, his hunger returned in full force.

"Unfortunately," she continued apologetically, "it will be Finding Fruit pudding. But the bedding is made of the best Cairntip doow duck down, and, once you burrow into that, I won't be seeing you awake any time soon, moons-light or not!"

The warm pudding turned out to be only slightly better than the raw fruit itself, so as Frankie nibbled at it, he used his imagination to transform the mushy substance into warm rice pudding sprinkled with sugar

and cardamom, an Indian dish that his father whipped up on holidays.

"Nice," Ideth praised him with relish. "I can smell the heavenly aroma. Am I right, or am I right?"

They ate the pudding off two delicate plates in the circle of light thrown by Ideth's hurricane lamp, surrounded by the ungainly shadows it created on the curved cave walls. The moons-light was much gentler now that the moons were overhead. The opening to the cave was shaded. By the time they were done eating and Ideth had rinsed and dried the dishes, the cave was almost dark, and Frankie was grateful to crawl into his ducky sack and close his eyes.

Ideth settled into her own, and soon they were side-by-side.

Ideth confided, "It's not a swimsuit. I never wear clothes if I can help it. Too much fuss. I like to travel light. What appears to be a swimsuit to you is a layer of blubber to keep me warm and buoyant in the sea. It's a part of my body. I can't take it off."

Frankie contemplated this.

"My mom hates the fat around her belly. She's always on a diet to lose weight."

"I can't imagine why," Ideth said, as she yawned and turned over on her side. "The more blubber the better, I say, especially for folks like us, whose ancestors evolved by the sea. And going on a diet? Are you kidding? Why on urth would anyone want to do that?"

6

Out to the Beach

deth was awake and puttering as soon as the first rays of sunlight filtered into the cave. She'd fashioned a broom from Finding Tree branches and was sweeping: *Scrape, scrape, scrape, scrape, scrape, scrape.* Then she started moving pots about: *Bang, clatter, "oops!" Clatter, BANG, "darn it!"*

A fire was next, and, after several attempts, it flamed to life. Then there was a crackling and popping sound as Ideth crawled through the small cave opening, disappearing briefly before returning with her largest cooking pot brimming with water: *Swing, swing, slush.*

She did all this with a kind of hush-hush, as if she were trying very hard not to wake up Frankie. But it was no good. Frankie came to consciousness as the muted noises continued, and grew annoyed as he dropped off to sleep one moment only to be awakened the next. For a boy who preferred to sleep until noon, it was a bit much. Ideth's obvious attempts *not* to wake him only made her behavior more irritating, and, after a few minutes, he gave up and decided it was better to get up altogether. Besides, was Ideth making breakfast? He suspected she was, and he immediately took interest.

When Ideth noticed he was awake, she said, "Finding Fruit oatmeal. And this is the last day of it, thank goodness."

Frankie wanted his usual breakfast of sweet cereal piled high with bananas, so he wasn't excited by the gunk Ideth spooned onto his plate. But he dove in anyway, grateful that it was food at all, for as soon as he saw it, he was famished.

When breakfast was over, Ideth efficiently cleaned up the dishes.

"You can wipe if you like, Frankie," she said, offering him a small dishtowel.

Frankie frowned. Was Ideth going to be just like his parents, nagging him to help?

"I need to pee," he muttered, heading for the mouth of the cave.

In Frankie's experience (which was quite extensive), going to the bathroom was a good excuse to duck out of work. No one could argue with it. And his need to relieve himself was true for once, so he took care of his business behind a boulder without one thought to Ideth and the clean-up from breakfast.

The morning air was crisp and delightful, and there was no sound except the muffled movement of Ideth inside the cave. The beauty of the trees in the sunlight, with their low-hanging round purple fruit, made Frankie happy. He sat down on a nearby rock, picked up a stick, and traced letters in the dirt.

FRANKIE, he wrote. TEN MEDALS! Then he scratched that out, grinning ear to ear, and wrote NO SCHOOL.

Frankie spent the next half-hour idly scratching and erasing words in the dirt, oblivious to his surroundings. Meanwhile, Ideth was busy packing, planning the day ahead. There was a lot to get into her backpack—two ducky sacks, two books, several pairs of reading glasses, a sewing kit, a first aid kit, some toiletries, the hurricane lantern, utensils, and her cooking gear. Her cooking pots nested inside one another (even the teapot, which fit snuggly inside the innermost pot), so, in the end, her pack was surprisingly tidy and compact. She was careful with her plates. They were family heirlooms and very dear to her. She tucked them inside the ducky sacks for protection. Then she cinched up the pack and hefted it onto her back, ready to go. On her way out, she dumped some water on the fire and grabbed her flare, which she would send up as soon as they reached the beach.

When Ideth emerged from the cave, Frankie had just scratched out SWING! and was about to write KING OF THE PERPLE FRUIT MONKEYS!

Ideth's eyes lit up. "King? I'm impressed! But you're about to misspell purple. It's PURPLE, not PERPLE. Am I right, or am I right?"

The shore was miles away, at the end of a complicated series of crisscrossed trails that Ideth seemed to know by heart. But it was a rather dull hike for Frankie because, other than the occasional large field of boulders and streams to cross, it was just one Finding Fruit tree after another. There were no lakes to swim in or animals to see or interesting things to pick up along the way, and, because he was wearing only socks (having left his shoes in Monterey), his feet got pretty beat up.

But Frankie kept going, hanging onto Ideth's promise of a beach at the end of their trek. And sure enough, after what seemed like an eon, he heard the distant sound of surf and crying seabirds. The forest thinned as the trail began a series of steep downhill switchbacks. At the bottom, there was a flat area where the trail widened out and the hard ground turned to sand. A few moments later, like miners crawling out from a dark chasm into the light of day, he and Ideth were standing on the edge of an expansive beach under a wide blue sky.

The shoreline down the street from Frankie's fine house in Monterey was rocky, and the water was ice cold. Even the nearby sandy beaches were chilly. He'd never seen a tropical beach before, with unbroken seashells littered about as if no one had ever gone beachcombing. Giant green tortoises lumbered slowly up and down the beach, stopping now and then at tidepools to hunt for food. It was odd, Frankie thought, that Urth tortoises lived on the beach. On Earth, they lived inland, leaving the sea for turtles. But there they were, plain as day. And something else confused him, too. The tide was *way* out. The damp sand a few feet ahead of them marked the high tide line. It seemed impossible that the ocean had receded to such a degree, but there was no doubt that it had.

"We're in a syzygy," Ideth explained. "The tides are extreme because our sun and both moons are aligned. The sun is on one side of Urth while our moons are both on the other side. Your planet only has one moon, so your tides aren't as dramatic. It's low tide now, but in about six hours, the ocean will sweep in and cover the beach altogether. I'm sorry you won't be able to witness it, but we'll be long gone by then.

Ideth led Frankie along the beach toward a long, high pier that stretched across the wet sand to where the surf was, in the distance. It was an amazing piece of engineering, but even so, Frankie was a little fearful, being scared of heights. However, Ideth helped him, and he managed to climb up a steep ladder without too much trouble. They reached the top and then walked several hundred feet before Ideth stopped and lit the flare. She appeared to know exactly what she was doing; the flare shot high into the azure, moons-less sky, arched motionless for a moment or two, and then lazily zig-zagged toward the horizon until it disappeared.

"Each uppy has her own flare color," she explained, "and there are up to a dozen of us on a finding at any given time. Mine is maroon to distinguish it from the flares of other uppies."

A long, high pier stretched across the sand to where the surf was…

"Is someone looking for it?" Frankie asked.

"Yes. There's a boatman out there, maybe half a mile out to sea. A fellow called Laup. You'll like him. When he sees the maroon flare, he'll know it's me and that I've found a child. He'll come pick us up."

Reaching the end of the pier took many more minutes because it was so long and Frankie stopped often. There were dozens of different kinds of crabs scuttling sidewise along the beach at amazing speeds, scampering toward the pier, briefly disappearing beneath it, and then racing out the other side. Below the pier, tortoises eyed him curiously, turning their less-than-graceful heads skyward before returning to their slow trudging. Hundreds of shorebirds skittered about feasting on crustaceans and other goodies brought in and dropped by the tide. And there was *sound*. Lots of it. After the silence of the Finding Forest, Frankie found it invigorating. The symphony of rolling surf, squawking birds, scuttling crabs, and gusty wind lifted his spirits.

At one point, Frankie looked behind him and gasped in awe at the beauty of the dense Finding Forest. It glittered in the sunshine along the entire shoreline, offering up its purple fruit like showy flowers.

Frankie wished he had his cell phone to take a photo and text it to his mom. She could spend hours in a place like this, snapping pictures of the forest from different angles to get just the right shot. Once, she'd taken a photo of him while he was sleeping that had won an award in the local newspaper. His classmates had teased him about it for a long time.

When they reached the end of the pier, the water was nearly up to the walkway and its color had deepened from a luminous turquoise to a majestic navy.

Ideth swept her arms to embrace the whole scene. "Isn't it stunning, Frankie? I'm so sorry your mother can't take a photo of it. Am I right, or am I right?"

"Do you have a cell phone?" Frankie asked hopefully. "Maybe I could use yours."

"Hmmm..." she replied, deep in thought. "You know,

my ancestors had something like your cell phones. They called them chatterboxes, I believe. But we lost the CB towers in the Great Melt a long time ago, and no one has rebuilt them."

A shadow passed over Ideth's face. The Great Melt had changed Urth forever and caused untold suffering. In a matter of decades, the polar ice caps had melted, and Urth's great continents and mountain ranges had been flooded. Now, only the tips of the mountain ranges remained, tiny islands above the otherwise endless sea. She tried not to think about the catastrophe and all the people who'd died. No one on Urth liked to talk about it. Now that the disaster was over, and the descendants of the survivors had created a new way of life, there seemed to be no point.

"But how do you communicate?" Frankie asked. "Everyone on Earth has a cell phone, even people who herd goats for a living. I've seen them on TV."

Ideth recovered her composure quickly. "We have paddle-saddlers who carry messages between islands, and, as you've seen, we also use flares. Some people swear by carrier gulls, but I've found them unreliable. A couple of years back, one flew off with my paycheck!"

"Sounds super slow."

"The paddle-saddlers are amazing athletes. They can paddle a message from Cairntip to Finding Island in only a few days. But you're right. Compared to chatterboxes and cell phones, I guess our methods take a long time."

Ideth paused and then added, "Some folks on Cairntip want so speed things up again. They're ambitious for their kids and push them hard. It's all about the future for them, and how to get the kids there as quickly as possible. I feel sorry for the children. I really do."

Frankie pondered this. His brother couldn't live without his many devices. Alex was always texting his friends and uploading photos onto social media. They'd gone camping once and Alex had gone through "withdrawal" as his mother had called it. But Frankie had climbed trees and watched herons fishing in the streams, happier than he'd ever been at the fine house by the sea with all its fancy technology. Some of the fantasies he'd enjoyed on that trip were worth repeating, with additional fun twists and turns, of course.

"In any case, no cell phone could capture this lovely view with all the sounds and smells that go with it," Ideth said. "Enjoy it now, before the boat comes."

Frankie didn't need any encouragement. He took a deep breath of the fresh sea air and raced down the remainder of the pier, turning several cartwheels. Then he turned around and cartwheeled back.

When he reached Ideth, breathless, he cried, "I'm a famous acrobat! I've just finished a show with the Urth Circus and am off for a grand tour of all the islands!"

Ideth grinned. She liked it when her findlings gave voice to their imaginings.

She thought, "It's no good for children like Frankie

to keep their wonderful daydreams locked up in their heads where no one else can enjoy them. After all, most people can't read minds."

Frankie did a few somersaults and then tried a gymnastic flip, which ended with an awkward half-dive off the peer into the water. He sputtered to the surface.

Ideth was concerned. "Are you all right?" she asked, hurrying over.

Frankie grinned. "See? I'm an expert pier diver, too. In fact, I'm the captain of the Finding Island Pier Diving Team!"

Ideth helped him back onto the pier.

A tad annoyed, she brushed off the wet mix of sand and salt water as best she could. "Well, you've made a mess of your Earth clothes. Why you bother to wear them is a puzzle to me."

He corrected her. "These aren't my Earth clothes. I'm wearing my pier diving uniform. And a pier diving uniform is supposed to get wet and dirty."

Ideth laughed.

"Let's make sure to tell Laup that or he'll think I'm neglecting you. We uppies are supposed to take care of our findlings, not let them get filthy. A pier diving outfit it is."

7

Laup

deth was right about Laup. Less than an hour after she'd shot off the flare, she and Frankie were climbing onto the deck of his small sailboat. Laup was a friendly, elderly Urth man who was clearly the skipper and sole shipmate to himself, wind-weathered and strong.

"Greetings and welcome, welcome!" he cried cheerily as he helped Ideth off with her backpack and onto a seat behind the mainsail. "You've had some luck, I see."

He turned to Frankie, looking him up and down with unbridled enthusiasm.

"Hello, findling!"

Frankie grinned. He liked Laup instantly.

Laup continued, "Welcome to Urth, and let me tell you, son, you landed on both feet. Ideth is one of the Uppy Council's finest. Why, she's completed thirty-two findings. Imagine that. Thirty-two! And you'll be her next successful one, I shouldn't wonder."

"Tut! Tut!" Ideth scolded. "I'm not anything special. Everyone plays a role in a finding, uppies like me and boatmen like you. Everyone knows that."

Laup turned to Frankie with a lopsided smile. "Don't listen to her boy. I'm just an old salt and she's an uppy."

Laup slapped Frankie on the back, as if he were an old sea buddy, and then asked, "Well, you're off to Krog Pad, eh? You'll have a grand time there, and that's the truth. It's been more than a year since I visited those folks and I miss them. They always make me laugh."

In overall appearance, Laup was much like Ideth. His skin was purple (a slightly darker shade than hers). His feet were webbed, his hair was long and thick, and he had a shimmering layer of blubber that looked like a swimsuit. But unlike Ideth, he wasn't fully naked. He was wearing a bright yellow loincloth.

Once Laup had gotten Ideth and Frankie comfortably seated, he opened a hatch, disappeared below, and reappeared with a picnic basket brimming with food.

"I expect you're both more than ready for some of this," he smiled, placing it before them. "Time to clean your palette of Finding Fruit."

Frankie couldn't wait to see what goodies were inside, but he sensed that he should hold back.

Laup saw the look of hesitation in Frankie's eyes and nodded approvingly. "That's it, boy. It's Ideth who gets the first dip. Let her take what she likes and you can have the rest. There's plenty for you both."

Ideth was already exploring the basket, and it wasn't long before she'd whipped out her special plates and heaped them with strange concoctions that smelled heavenly.

Ideth handed Frankie his plate and he gobbled down every bite. He had no idea what he was eating, but after the Finding Fruit he didn't much care.

When they were thoroughly stuffed and the goodness of the food was seeping into their blood, Laup put the leftovers to one side while Ideth cleaned her precious plates with sea water and carefully dried them before slipping them back into her pack.

Laup asked, "Is there anything you're missing? My hold is full of the usual stuff."

"Frankie was sunburned in outer space, so if you have any bitter bugger spray, we could use some. Other than that, we'll travel light. Just wrap up those leftovers so we have something to eat for lunch and bring up the paddling supplies. That should do it."

"Leftovers *and* a cure for those Krog Padders!" Laup laughed, shaking his head as he disappeared again below deck.

Frankie could hear him rummaging around. A minute or two later, he reemerged, dragging a round object behind him by a rope, *bump! bump! bump!* up the stairs. It was the paddling buoy, about the size of a beach ball.

"Nice and roomy," he said, breathing heavily and dropping his burden on the deck. "A bit of a beast, but it's watertight, guaranteed. Let's get your belongings inside."

Laup unlatched the buoy's curved door and carefully placed Ideth's backpack within. He knew she was sensitive about her fancy plates, and didn't want to break them.

"And we'll need those clothes of yours," Laup told Frankie. "Otherwise, your wet suit won't fit properly."

Frankie looked at Ideth in alarm.

"I have to take off my clothes?" he thought loudly, opening his eyes wide and looking straight into hers.

It was the first time he'd tried to communicate to her through his mind, and it worked just fine.

Ideth told him, "Just down to your underwear. I know you findlings don't like going naked."

Frankie reluctantly removed his t-shirt, shorts, and soggy socks before he remembered that he was wearing a pair of Mickey Mouse boxers underneath. He'd put them on back home, never dreaming anyone would see them. They were two sizes too small (they belonged to Alex) and made him look like he was only six or seven. Embarrassing.

Whether out of politeness or simply because they didn't notice, Ideth and Laup didn't comment on his boxers. Instead, Laup handed him some bitter bugger spray, which he smeared on his skin while Laup and Ideth worked together to fill the buoy and seal it up.

"Pier diving suit," Ideth informed Laup casually, as they rolled Frankie's clothes military-fashion, as was the custom at sea. "That's why they're such a mess. Supposed to be filthy, you know."

When they were done, Laup fastened down the latch, slapping the side of the buoy with pride. "Now for the harness."

The harness was similar to those used by mountain climbers. Ideth wriggled into it, obviously an expert at hitching herself up.

"Thanks. Fits perfectly."

Laup grinned and turned to Frankie.

"Go choose a wetsuit while I find you a mask and snorkel. I've got several suits to choose from, just 'round the starboard side."

Frankie pawed through the rack of suits and quickly selected a silver and black one with a shark emblazoned on the side.

"I like this one," he said.

As he stared at the shark, he imagined himself riding it, a whip in his hand, bucking through the waves. He was a seafaring rancher herding a pod of porpoises. He urged his shark on with a slap to the flanks. The shark responded and picked up speed.

"Lovely, lovely!" Ideth clapped, her face brightening. "You'd make a fine porpoise-boy, Frankie. But I'm afraid that wetsuit is a bit big. You need one that's nice and snug or it won't keep you warm and buoyant. You

might go into hypothermia otherwise, or find yourself struggling to stay afloat."

Frankie put the wetsuit back reluctantly but soon found another that was just as appealing. It was blood red in color and displayed a large, scary octopus on the back. Once he'd pulled it on (which took some time because it was awkward and rubbery), he sat down, waiting for Laup to start the boat and whisk them away to Krog Pad, which was apparently their destination. The fact that the snorkel and mask that Laup had given him were lying, unused, on his lap didn't faze him. He figured they were for use later, on Krog Pad, snorkeling in shallow waters.

Reading his mind, Ideth immediately set him straight.

"We're not going to bother Laup for a ride to Krog Pad Island. He's got other uppies to help. We're going to paddle there, and you'll need the snorkel and mask for that. Krog Pad is sixty miles from here."

"Swimming," Laup interjected. "Paddling is swimming."

Frankie was temporarily stunned, a feeling that quickly turned to fear.

"We're going to SWIM?" he asked aloud. When he got to the word "SWIM," he opened his eyes so wide that they looked like Ideth's dinner plates.

"Yes, and you'll need to follow my directions to stay safe. That being said, I haven't lost a findling yet. But we'd better get started or we'll miss dinner at the East

End Paddling Station, which would be a shame. The chef there is excellent."

Laup added, "The East End Paddling Station is midway to Krog Pad, Frankie. You don't have to paddle the sixty miles in one stretch. Still, you'll need to cover thirty today, which is a lot for a first-time paddler. It's lucky you have such nice weather. In a storm, it might take you a week."

Frankie panicked. When his parents had taught him to swim in the family pool when he was a toddler ("We want to make sure you can swim out if you fall in"), he'd barely learned the basics. Since then, the neighbor's kids, Andreas and Paulo, had earned spots on the regional water polo team, the Central Coast Squids. Frankie hadn't even tried out. Now, he faced swimming miles and miles in *open ocean* on a planet where the people were even better swimmers than Andreas and Paulo! Ideth and Laup must think he was a super-swimmer, too. Likely all Urth children were.

A wave of hot fear took hold of him, and he thought, "I'll have to tell them the truth or I'll drown."

Ideth stepped in to offer some reassurance. "Not one of my former findlings could paddle when they got here. Children with the gift of *Fantasy* rarely know how to do practical things. But all of them survived their trip to Krog Pad. Of course, little Nathaniel almost got snatched by a dodecopus, but I rescued him in time. Biggest dodecopus I've ever seen. Quite impressive."

Ideth meant well, but her words only heightened Frankie's anxiety. He closed his eyes and fantasized himself losing his grip on Ideth's hair, swimming desperately to catch up with her—reaching out with both hands for her long ribbon of hair and barely missing—while a hungry dodecopus pursued him. He imagined the beast's nasty beak and enormous tentacles. It would crush him in moments, spewing blood into the current, attracting other dodecopuses. Ideth would suddenly notice she'd lost him and flounder around, searching for him without success.

By the end of the day, he'd be dead, 64,000 light years from home. And there was nothing, it seemed, that Ideth or Laup were going to do about it!

8

Paddling with Ideth

F rankie had been snorkeling once in Hawaii, but only very close to shore in ridiculously safe conditions. He needed a brief reminder on how to use a snorkel (which he only half-listened to because he was so frightened) and additional instructions concerning how to *hold on*.

"You grasp it here," Ideth demonstrated, kneeling down to his level. She grabbed his left hand and buried it firmly into a coarse tuft of hair that protruded from the backside of her scalp. It had a different texture than the rest of her long hair. Apparently, it had a special purpose.

"That's the target," she instructed. "A firm grasp with your left hand is what's needed. You'll paddle to my right."

Frankie let go and Ideth deftly dove off the deck into the water. The buoy was already floating nearby, and she came up gracefully next to it. She clipped the end of the buoy's rope to her harness. She was ready to go.

Laup said to Frankie, "Now it's your turn. I'll help."

Laup took Frankie to the back of the boat and demonstrated how to lower himself into the ocean without getting water into his snorkel.

Frankie's heart was thumping in his chest, but Ideth reached out for him calmly, with an encouraging smile, and he eased himself into the water without mishap. To his surprise, the wetsuit kept him afloat without much effort on his part. He was buoyant, just as Ideth had promised. Just a gentle back-and-forth motion with his legs was sufficient to keep his head above water. It was a great relief.

"Remember, grab my tuft with your left hand, and paddle to my right. Three tugs say 'trouble,' one tug says 'okay.' If you want to surface for a rest, tug twice. We'll be surfacing every so often so I can breathe. Follow my lead. I'll do all the work."

Frankie grabbed Ideth's tuft with both hands, and she gently corrected him.

"Just the left hand, Frankie. That's it. Try to relax if you can. It's like floating. You'll find that the tuft grabs onto your hand just as hard as you grab onto it. The tufts evolved so our children could hold on while we paddle. They serve their purpose well."

Frankie grasped the tuft as directed and suddenly found himself underwater. For a moment, the world was a swirl of liquid murkiness. But then he felt a gentle tug, and his body straightened out, just under the waves, his snorkel clearing the surface of the water like a periscope.

Thrust, thrust, float.

Ideth took her first strokes.

Frankie mentally checked in. His left hand was grabbing Ideth's tuft. *Or was the tuft grabbing him?* His mouth was sealed around the mouthpiece of the snorkel; no leaks. Ideth was just beneath him, off to his left, her black hair streaming during the thrust, thrust, and drifting during the float.

"Three tugs say 'trouble,' one tug says 'okay.' If you want to surface for a rest, tug twice." Frankie repeated the instructions to himself four times in a row, just to be sure he knew them by heart, and then tugged once.

They were off.

Have you ever gone swimming in the ocean with your eyes open and a big breath of air in your lungs? If so, I hope it was a warm ocean. In a warm ocean the water is only a bit cooler than your own body, and it feels like a second skin. You feel like you're part of something huge and majestic, much bigger than yourself.

When Frankie had snorkeled in Hawaii, it had been so baby-like—presented in a pseudo-laidback style. The instructor had shown the kids photographs of fish and set up a prize system to reward the "top three" children who could identify them in their first practice session. Mothers and fathers had hovered nearby on the shore, waving encouragingly while their children entered the water. Frankie was sure that the parents had pretended, to one another, that they didn't care whether their child was one of the "top three," when, in truth, they cared a great deal.

Frankie's experience paddling with Ideth couldn't have been more different. It was *real*. It was *adult*. There was at least fifty feet of water between him and the ocean floor below, and if he got separated from Ideth, he was sure he'd drown or get eaten. It was do or die: grab Ideth's tuft with his left hand and breathe deeply through his snorkel, or get carried off by the swells. He'd only known his uppy for less than twenty-four hours, and though he liked her, he didn't know if he could trust her. He wouldn't know until the paddle was over and he was safe.

Frankie tugged twice, and they surfaced. There was an awkward moment while he spat out his snorkel.

"I just wanted to make sure two tugs worked," he said.

Ideth took several very long, deep breaths, using the opportunity to refresh her oxygen supply.

She nodded approvingly and said, "Good for you. You need to confirm that you understand the rules properly. Gives you confidence."

They bobbed on the surface for a minute or two, but there was nothing much to see. The ocean stretched off in all directions with no sight of land. Frankie fought down a sudden panic.

"I'm going to start navigating," Ideth told him. "It will feel strange. I'll be sending out sound waves so I can see the ocean floor around us."

"Like radar?" Frankie asked, nervously.

"Exactly." Ideth was impressed her findling understood the main principle of echolocation. "The thing is, you won't be able to hear the sounds I make. They're out of range of your hearing. You'll *feel* them. You'll see once we get going again."

Frankie put his snorkel back in his mouth and straightened it. Then he tugged once on Ideth's tuft. Ideth took in another big breath, let out about half of it, and then dropped beneath the waves.

A few moments later, Frankie felt a tingling sensation ripple through his skin. Ideth was navigating. As they paddled along, the tingling came and went as Ideth "echo-visualized" the landscape of the ocean floor beneath them, and led them expertly in the direction of the East End Paddling Station. It was a route she seemed to know well.

There's no way I can do justice to the colors, sizes, and numbers of fish that Frankie saw as they paddled their way east that day. Sometimes a school would appear suddenly and surround them, and the next moment it would be gone. Most of the action was on the reef below, and Frankie eventually relaxed enough to forget about the risk of drowning and enjoy the show.

There was only one time that he almost tugged on Ideth's tuft three times, in alarm, but the massive purple shark passed before he had time to do it. It took several minutes for the aftermath of the sudden stab of adrenalin to go away.

Around noon, they stopped for a quick lunch. When they'd set out, he hadn't considered how they would eat on the go. With a full belly, it's hard to imagine having an empty one, and by the time you do, it's hard to imagine it was ever full. When Ideth stopped paddling and retrieved their leftover breakfast from the buoy, his stomach grumbled.

What follows is an abbreviated account of the sloppy, watery lunch that ensued as they bobbed about in the open ocean: *Yuk*. It wasn't much, and Frankie was almost as hungry afterwards as he'd been when they'd started. But it was something rather than nothing, and it would have to do.

Thrust, thrust, float. Thrust, thrust, float. Thrust, thrust, float. The journey seemed to go on forever.

At first, paddling was a lot like learning to ride a bike. Frankie had to concentrate very hard to get it right. He was sure his mask would fill up with water sooner or later, or that Ideth's tuft would suddenly let him go. But eventually, he trusted the process and his imagination took over. He whipped up some wonderful fantasies—richly embellished ones where he played the role of a plundering pirate of the East Seas, a coral miner with a

As the sun set, the water turned a deep blue-gold...

large underwater flashlight and a huge pick axe, and a castaway who was really a spy.

As the afternoon went on, the sun gradually made its way toward the western horizon behind them. The water turned a deep blue-gold. Frankie was starting to think that Ideth was lost, when she surfaced and did her deep breathing routine one last time. When she'd topped herself off with oxygen she said, "About five minutes now. We're almost there."

They returned to paddling and, just as promised, the East End Paddling Station came into view a few minutes later.

"It's more like a submarine than a station," thought Frankie as Ideth swerved to avoid hitting one of the mighty cables that held the station in place.

The underground portion of the building was four stories high and brightly painted. A mural of colorful ocean creatures covered one wall, while another sported a youthful Urth woman offering up a conch full of food. As they swam closer, the details of the building came into view, and Frankie could see a line of portholes on each floor.

Ideth paddled them over to a broad ladder, which extended several feet into the water from a platform above. When they reached it, she helped Frankie get his footing and then gave his bottom a boost so he could grab the rails. The platform rocked and it took Frankie two tries to get out of the water and onto the deck. But once he was safe, he was able to sit down, remove his mask and snorkel, shake the water out of his hair, and look around.

Ideth was close on his heels.

"Well done, findling," she said, as she plopped down beside him. "You've completed your first paddle. What do you think?"

Frankie grinned, relieved it was all over. He was about to tell her about the shark, and how he'd barely escaped its jaws (a wild exaggeration which she would have loved), but he was interrupted before he could begin.

A young Urth woman in a crisp white uniform had seen them arrive and walked up to them with a clipboard.

"I hope you have a reservation," she said hesitantly. "I'm afraid we're not taking paddle-bys any longer. The East Ender's in high demand, you know."

Ideth got to her feet. She was several inches shorter than the woman, but it hardly mattered. Looking up at her she said, "Is Mot here? He's the boss and he'll tell you. I don't need a reservation. I'm an uppy."

"Oh, I didn't realize who you were..." the woman said, backing away to a respectful distance. For the first time, she took notice of Frankie and could see, without a doubt, that he was an Earth child. "The East Ender always holds back rooms for important guests like you."

More gently, Ideth replied, "I'm a regular here, but I don't believe we've met before. You must be new."

The woman nodded. Ideth's expression was friendly and warm, and she opened up.

"Mot's on Cairntip right now," she admitted. "He's left me in charge. Imagine that. With no experience. I only started last week, and one of the guests is giving me no end of trouble."

Ideth was sympathetic. "I'm sorry to hear that. It's always difficult starting a new job. Lots to get used to. But you'll be fine once you get the hang of things. Mot's a fair boss and a kind one, if a bit confused at times."

The woman looked relieved.

"In any event," Ideth continued, "we'd like to freshen up in time for dinner, so I hope it's not too much trouble to get our buoy stowed and our belongings brought to our cabin in a jiffy. We've just paddled thirty miles from Finding Island, and though Frankie is an expert pier diver, I'm afraid we're both a bit done in."

9

A Berth at the East Ender

T he East End Paddling Station, it turned out, was an underwater hotel. Once Frankie saw the set-up, and realized they'd be sleeping beneath the waves, he was thrilled. The "above board" floor of the station was a reception area enclosed by a glass dome that looked as if it had seen better days. But it was a hotel in the middle of the ocean, after all, and got pooped on by sea birds and weathered by wind and rain. Someone had affixed a stuffed owl to the top of the dome in a futile attempt to keep the birds away, but there was a gull preening its feathers, perched atop the owl's fuzzy head.

Ideth snorted in amusement. "It's a Cairntip gull-eating owl. And you can see all the bloody good the fake owl is doing to keep the gulls away."

The woman with the clipboard introduced herself as

"A Nice Gal."

"What a funny name," Frankie thought.

"I'll explain later," Ideth whispered. "Her name isn't as strange as it may seem, at least not here on Urth."

A Nice Gal led them to the front desk and scanned the guest list. She pretended to be searching for a spare room, when in fact there were many. Mot had directed her to always make it seem that the hotel was full, but her charade didn't fool Ideth. When she looked up, she saw the amusement in Ideth's eyes and she smiled back, sheepishly.

"One room, twin berths, ocean view. One uppy and one findling. I'll put you in the Seahorse Room."

A Nice Gal directed a teenage boy to secure their buoy, whispering "Uppy and findling. Get moving!" under her breath. Then the boy unloaded their belongings into a large plastic "guest tub," and disappeared down a staircase at the back of the reception building.

"Dinner's included for findlings," she continued, as if reciting instructions, word-for-word, from the East End Paddling Station's Rules and Regulations (which she was). Then, looking directly at Ideth, she added, "And your stay, madam, is entirely free. We won't be charging the Uppy Council a single Cairntip tidbit for the honor of having you as our guest."

The staircase connected the above-board floor with the cabins below. Before he followed Ideth down, Frankie glanced into the Station dining room, where there was a long table covered with white linen. A white-board announced, "Dinner served promptly at seven. Loincloths respectfully suggested."

Their room was even more fun and intriguing than Frankie had imagined. The walls were covered with murals of seahorses, and the shelves were lined with books about them: *All the Urth's Seahorses, Seahorses of the Southern Islands, My Mommy's a Seahorse!*

Along one side of the room was a set of bunkbeds, each bed with a porthole at the pillow end so the occupant could see out.

"We're at sea, so our beds are called berths," Ideth said. "Would you like the top berth or the bottom?"

"The top berth," Frankie replied. "But I'm sopping wet."

"Yes, that's a problem, but with an easy solution. I'll give your pier diving suit to the staff to launder. In the meantime, I'll borrow some loincloths from the East Ender's supply. They rent them out to visitors because they want everyone to dress for dinner. It's an unnecessary tradition in my view, but I always comply to be polite. I'll see if I can find a pair of sandals for you, too. It's dangerous to go barefoot at a paddling station. Loose nails. Too bad you left your shoes at home."

Ideth disappeared briefly, returning only a few minutes later with two loincloths (a green one for Frankie and a blue one for herself), and a pair of beach sandals.

Ideth laughed. "I think more than a few findlings

have borrowed these over the years, but they'll do in a pinch. They're made to fit human feet, and they look to be about the right size for you."

There was a small bathroom in their quarters with just enough room for Frankie to remove his wetsuit and boxers, take a quick shower ("Scrub!" shouted Ideth from behind the closed door), and don the loincloth. But putting on the odd outfit was difficult for him. He had never worn a loincloth before and had no idea how to loop it around and secure it. The longer he worked at folding it around his midsection and up through his legs, the more confused he became.

He called out in frustration, "Need help! But don't look!"

"Oh, you needn't be so shy," Ideth replied dismissively. "I know all about your anatomy. But I know you humans like your privacy, so I'll just demonstrate the process on myself. It's easy once you see someone else do it."

Frankie stuck his head out from behind the bathroom door to watch. Ideth picked up her own loincloth, shook it out, and then showed Frankie, step-by-step, how to put it on.

"Where are Ideth's private parts?" he wondered. "Maybe she doesn't have any."

Having read his thoughts, she explained. "They're up inside, beneath our blubber, where you can't see them. That's why we don't care about going naked. No one can see anything, anyway. Am I right, or am I right?"

Frankie disappeared into the bathroom and re-emerged about two minutes later, his loincloth hanging just as it should.

Ideth stood back and admired him as the station swayed ever so slightly beneath their feet.

"You're starting to look like a native," she said, smiling. "I'll take my shower now, and you can explore your berth. I'll be out soon."

Frankie climbed the bunkbed ladder and peered through the porthole. It was getting dark, and he couldn't see much. Suddenly, though, a row of external floodlights sputtered to life and gave him a view of some of the creatures lurking in the murky waters. A grouper swam up to the window and stared at him, hanging in the swaying water as if to appraise this new East End Paddling Station guest. Frankie tapped on the glass, which did not seem to impress the fish. It darted away almost instantly and disappeared into the blue beyond.

The berth was extremely comfortable.

As she came out of the bathroom, Ideth said, "The East Ender has the softest ducky sacks on Urth. I'm not sure who makes them, but they're like sinking into butter."

She lay down on her own berth for a "quick bit of shut-eye" while Frankie flopped on his back and put his legs straight up into the air. He could flatten his heels against the ceiling with his legs in that position, and getting them upside down felt very refreshing after the long day's paddle. He hadn't done much of the hard work, of course, but he was tired nonetheless.

"I'm the captain of this paddling station," he imagined. "A *pirate* captain who sails the high seas in search of loot: gold, silver, and precious jewels."

He envisioned himself with a black patch over one eye and a peg leg: *Long Frankie Silver,* supreme captain of his own vessel, the Ship of East Ends. Ideth would be an assistant pirate, waiting on him hand and foot. Below deck there would be dangerous comrades with gold teeth and missing fingers. Chained, angry dogs. An ugly black tom cat with only one eye. What fun!

His mind wandered for the next half hour, engaged in other delightful flights of fancy, but the sound of a loud gong finally interrupted his reverie, and the colorful images in his mind faded away.

"That's the dinner bell," Ideth said enthusiastically, sitting up so suddenly that she banged her head on the underside of Frankie's berth.

"Ouch!" she cried, rubbing her head testily. "I *always* seem to do that when I sleep here. Why do my findlings choose the top berth every time? There's nothing special about it."

Frankie climbed down, feeling a tad guilty. Ideth was tired from the paddle, no doubt, and now she'd bumped her head.

"And, by the way," Ideth said, "I don't much like being assigned the role of assistant pirate, where I'd be

nothing but a slave. I wasn't asleep just now. I was just resting and I could read your mind just fine."

"Okay," Frankie readily agreed. "In my next fantasy, you can be a co-pirate. But be sure to bring a treasure map. You'll have to earn your keep!"

10

Shum

Despite A Nice Gal's attempts to make it appear otherwise, the hotel was lightly populated. There were only two other guests, to be exact. One was a trader named Watler from Cairntip, who was selling Finding Fruit ("the best this side of Finding Island") in exchange for almost anything else.

"No takers here," Ideth told him, winking at Frankie. "We've had enough of that dreadful stuff to last a lifetime."

The other guest was a goofy-looking man named Shum who grinned at them with his tongue hanging out, and had to be calmed down several times (though not unkindly) by A Nice Gal, who'd shed her role as concierge and was now doubling as a waitress.

"Let's *leave it* for now, Shum," she chastised him repeatedly.

Shum responded by bouncing up and down in his chair, joyously shouting, "Happy be! Food for me!"

Frankie was immediately entranced and found himself bouncing, too. Shum looked much like Ideth and Laup. He was clearly of the same species, but his exuberant behavior was markedly different from theirs.

"Shum's on his way back home to Krog Pad tomorrow, thank goodness," A Nice Gal whispered to Ideth. "I've had just about as much of that duppy as I can stand."

On deck, A Nice Gal had been perky, but she appeared haggard now.

"Don't I know it," Ideth whispered back. "We'll be on Krog Pad for the next few Lunera months at least, and I'm having to steel myself."

"I thought so," A Nice Gal replied, turning her gaze briefly in Frankie's direction. "The gift of *Fantasy*. You can see it in those eyes of his."

Frankie whispered to Ideth, "What's a duppy?"

"I'll tell you later," she whispered back.

There were no menus. A Nice Gal served their meal family style, with dishes appearing spontaneously at regular intervals and in no apparent order.

Ideth told Frankie, as she helped herself to some soup, "It doesn't matter where you start. You arrive in the same place: satisfied!"

Shum was beside himself with delight when the food arrived. He leapt up, nearly upsetting a steaming bowl of rice.

A Nice Gal sternly asked him to leave the table. "PLEASE, Shum! Give the others a chance to get started!"

Amazingly, Shum slunk away to stand at the far side of the room, looking remorseful, his eyes still fixed on the food. Only after Ideth, Watler, and Frankie had served themselves, did A Nice Gal permit Shum to return.

"Manners!" she hissed.

Shum calmed down as she heaped some food onto his plate.

"Been paddling for three weeks," Watler grumbled as he dug in. "The business was good at first but now it's fallen off. My buoy's still full of Finding Fruit and it's starting to rot. Shouldn't be telling you that, of course, but I can see you're fresh back from Finding Island and won't be interested."

"Me fruit have!" Shum shouted, jumping up once more. His chair fell backwards onto the floor and he grinned ecstatically. "Happy be!"

The waitress flew back into the room from the galley. "No, Shum. You don't want to sleep outside on the deck again, do you? You'll be forced to, you know, if you keep acting this way."

With a look of deep embarrassment, Shum slumped.

A Nice Gal turned to the other guests apologetically. "Mr. Shum has an excitable temperament, but a heart of gold."

Shum looked up tentatively and then broke into another wide grin.

"But you need to control yourself," she added, turning to look at him again, with a frown and one eyebrow raised. "Do we understand one another?"

She threw Ideth an exasperated glance as she cleared some of the bowls and prepared to bring in more.

"It's because they never get food like this on Krog Pad," Watler said. "No cooking."

Shum lowered his eyes.

"It's all right, fella," Watler went on, in a gentler tone. "Born into that culture. Never learned the value of a solid day's work."

"Every culture has its strengths and weaknesses," Ideth pointed out. "No people are as free-spirited as the Krog Padders. They know how to live in the here and now and enjoy life. They never fret and worry. Never."

Shum looked up, hopefully.

"Yes, I suppose that's right," said Watler. "And I realize you need to take the boy to Krog Pad." His eyes swept past Ideth and Shum to Frankie.

"We free!" cried Shum, alight again. "Happy be run! Beach be free!"

Watler piled a heap of food on his plate. "Yes, well. I'm just glad you have your own beaches and aren't running around on Cairntip's. No offense."

Shum slumped.

"Well, Watler, you can have your Cairntip beaches," said Frankie. "We're going to Krog Pad after we leave here, aren't we, Ideth? I want to run on the beach and play with *you*, Shum!"

Shum could barely contain himself, shaking with the effort to prevent himself from leaping up again. "We! We!" he gasped in short, staccato breaths, as he looked toward A Nice Gal, who was glowering at him.

After dinner, everyone stepped out onto the deck and watched the moons-rise. Ru, Urth's orange moon, rose first, followed by Lunera. Both were past full, no longer completely round the way they'd been when Frankie had first seen them, back in the Finding Forest.

"Waning gibbous phase," Ideth explained. "Soon the moons will pull apart. In a few days, Lunera won't be up in the evening sky any longer. By the time it's at third quarter, it won't rise until about midnight. Ru, on the other hand, will stick around longer. It passes through its phases more slowly because it's farther away."

Shum ran up and down the deck, pointing excitedly at the moons. He even leapt into the water at one point, rising happily to the surface with an enormous, goofy grin, as if Urth's moons were entirely new to him and beyond fabulous.

Ideth looked on in amusement. She thought (and not for the first time), "What odd people the Krog Padders are. But they make me smile. I have to admit it."

When they arrived back in their cabin, Ideth handed Frankie a sketch pad and a pencil.

"Do you like to draw?"

Frankie cocked his head to one side. He didn't think

he was very artistic—at least not on paper. All his images were stored in his head. But he decided to give it a try. It took him half an hour, but in the end, he'd completed a sketch of Ideth.

"Looks just like me," Ideth assured him, though she thought it made her look too skinny and a great deal too much like a duck.

They crawled into their berths to go to sleep.

Frankie spent half an hour or so with his nose pressed against the porthole, enjoying the parade of sea creatures now circling the hotel. He realized they were feeding off the refuse from dinner. As they passed him, he recognized some of the menu items he'd enjoyed earlier, dragging from their mouths.

Eventually, though, Frankie got sleepy and burrowed into his ducky sack. It didn't take long for the gentle *rock-rock, slush-slush* of the East End Paddling Station to lull him to sleep.

While he slept, his body lay in a berth at the East Ender, but his mind was on Krog Pad Island, where he was running down a sandy beach under an impossibly blue sky, his new friend Shum leaping enthusiastically beside him.

11

Frankie's Renaming

T he next morning, at breakfast, Shum was notably absent. When Frankie inquired about him, A Nice Gal explained, "He left early this morning. I filled up his buoy with food last night, hoping he'd take the hint."

Frankie was disappointed. Without Shum in the mix, the table conversation was dull. Ideth and Watler droned on about import taxes, politics, and the "ridiculously inflated" cost of inland caves on Cairntip. They were worried about stuff that bored him to tears.

Apparently, Urth people lived in caves as often as they lived in houses. And they had hefty mortgages that kept them up at night. Frankie wondered what it would be like to live in an Urth cave. Did caves have windows? How about electricity?

In his mind's eye, he spun up an image of a cave,

cushy like his house back home, with an induction stove and two servants to bring him his dinner every night, on schedule.

Frankie ate two helpings of everything and wandered back to the Seahorse Room. He wanted to text his friends and brag about his adventures, but his cell phone was back in Monterey, out of battery life, and in the hands of the police (though he didn't know that).

He didn't think of texting his poor parents, which I suppose is understandable given that he had no idea of the pain they were going through. Instead, he experimented with how long he could hold a headstand.

When Ideth found him, his record was more than fifteen seconds—not bad on a gently rocking floor. The only problem was that his loincloth flipped forward into his face when he was upside down. Even though his private parts were still covered (Urth loincloths manage that in all positions), he felt oddly exposed. When he heard Ideth coming down the hallway, he immediately shot up the ladder to his berth and pretended to examine a mole on his arm.

Moments later, the door swung open. "Fifteen seconds is astounding. My record is only five. Am I right, or am I right?"

Ideth headed to the bathroom and emerged, naked. "So much for loincloths. What a nightmare."

Frankie, keen to get off the subject of loincloths, said, "I miss Shum." He was curious about the delightful man, and wondered why he was going to Krog Pad to join him.

Ideth, reading his mind, said, "Remember when I told you have a mission here on Urth? Every findling has one, and children with the gift of *Fantasy* always carry them out on Krog Pad."

"Will it involve a monster?" Frankie asked eagerly.

"I have no idea," Ideth said. "In any event, you won't be missing Shum for long. If all goes well, we'll be seeing him before the day is out. No doubt he paddled straight to Krog Pad and is waiting for us already. There are no paddling stations between here and there, and even if there were, it's unlikely he'd be welcome. Most stations turn away Krog Padders. Too much trouble, especially at dinner."

Frankie couldn't imagine anyone disliking Shum. Watler was another story. He was a snooze. But Shum was as likeable as anyone could possibly be.

Ideth added briskly, "Anyway, before we pack up and leave, you need to choose a new name. A *rename*. We can't leave for Krog Pad until you've renamed yourself. Those are the rules."

Frankie sat up. Ideth hadn't told him about renaming yet.

"What's a rename?" he asked.

"It's a new name to replace Frankie," she explained. "All children must break free of their parents at some point, and here on Urth choosing your own name is the first step."

Frankie perked up. "On my planet, most kids don't get free of their parents until they go away to college."

"Understood," Ideth smiled, "but I think that's a bit too late, don't you?"

Frankie nodded enthusiastically. He couldn't have agreed more.

"I thought the idea would appeal to you," Ideth laughed. "So, let's get started. The weather report today isn't promising and we need to get a move on. I borrowed a bag of Renaming Letters from the station's stash. Mot always keeps a set on hand. It's time you got busy."

Ideth explained to Frankie that renaming was a ritual "as old as the sun, moons, and stars," and that while it had once been governed by a formal ceremony, the process these days was more relaxed.

Ideth handed Frankie the bag, which looked like it might belong to a magician. It was royal purple and inlaid with gemstones that formed strange, other-worldly symbols.

"This bag contains all the letters in the alphabet, many times over. Your job is to choose the letters in FRANKIE and shuffle them around to create an anagram. The anagram becomes your rename."

Frankie was confused, so Ideth continued. "You can't choose a rename willy-nilly. A boy named Muffin can't rename himself John, no matter how much he wishes he could. Instead, he's limited to the letters in his original name. He could be Niffum or Iffnum—both far better than Muffin, I think."

"And Bart could become Brat!" Frankie snickered, catching on.

"Exactly."

Frankie paused. A light went on in his head. "Is Ideth your rename?" he asked. "And what about A Nice Gal? I'll bet that's her rename, too!"

"That's right. A Nice Gal split her rename into more than one word, which children are permitted to do. It helps if you have a long birth name, like Angelica. Easier for folks to pronounce."

Frankie was especially eager to choose a rename when he learned that children have more control over their lives afterwards.

"After I renamed myself, I told my parents I was going to be an uppy," Ideth explained with a reminiscent smile. "They wanted me to join the family's tidal energy business, but I opted for fun and adventure over soulless labor."

"Happy be!" Frankie shouted, leaping off his berth, running around the room, mimicking Shum.

Ideth laughed. "There'll be plenty of time for that. Now come over here and get the bag of letters. Time to get busy."

Frankie took the bag, climbed back to his berth, and lay down on his stomach. The Renaming Letters were small squares of wood, about one inch on each

side. They looked a lot like Scrabble pieces but without the numbers. He dumped the letters onto his ducky sack and sorted through them to find the seven letters in FRANKIE. Then he shuffled them around with his fingers, considering each possibility in turn.

"FRANEIK, IEKFRAN, and KNARFIE," he said (or tried to say) to himself. "I don't think so."

"This is hard…'" he thought, gazing out his porthole. A barracuda appeared in the glass and then drained away.

He tried again, this time looking for familiar words, like a Scrabble player trying to make a play.

"FEAR INK," he giggled. "Not bad." He imagined himself leaping over tall buildings to escape from a giant ball point pen that was threatening to wipe out all humanity in a single stroke.

Ideth was packing up their things, but she was listening in. "Tut, tut," she said. "No war images." Then she asked, "Is Frankie your full name?"

"No, my real name's Francesco. After my granddad. He was Italian. But I never use it. I'm part Asian, too, a kind of a mix."

"Well, you might want to start using your Italian name," Ideth said. "You'll have more choices with a name like that, and maybe you'll hit on something special."

Francesco "Frankie" Russo considered this idea and decided to go for it. He selected the nine letters he needed and started the anagramming process again. Ideth was right. There were a lot more possibilities.

Sorting through them might take hours!

He was only a couple of minutes into his assignment when Ideth cried, "Oh, bother. I forgot your laundry. That won't do. Be right back."

She left the room, but Frankie was so absorbed in his work that he barely noticed she was gone.

CORN FACES. Frankie laughed as a cornfield popped into his mind, with scarecrows dotted here and there. Each scarecrow sported Shum's happy, goofy face, turned upward grinning into the bright sun.

"Cute, but maybe not," Frankie thought, scrambling the letters around again.

FORCE CANS.

He frowned. "No. There's gotta be something better than that!"

Several more possibilities presented themselves, and he dismissed them, too, one by one. After a time, he grew frustrated. At his lowest point, he almost decided on ARFCESCO just to be done. But finally, inspiration struck like a hammer hitting a nail dead-on.

"That's it!" he cried.

By the time Ideth returned to the Seahorse Room, Soccer Fan had printed out his new name in large letters on his sketch pad.

When she appeared in the doorway, he held it up for her to see.

Ideth's eyes lit up as she dropped Soccer Fan's clean clothes into the guest tub and clapped her hands

*Inspiration struck Frankie like a hammer
hitting a nail dead on...*

in approval. "I love it. Perfect choice. I know all about soccer from other findlings. Francesco came in handy, didn't it?"

Soccer Fan agreed. "My brother's Italian name is Alessandro, if you can believe that. I wonder what rename he'd choose."

"Maybe he'll find out one day. Meantime, do you play soccer back home?" Ideth asked.

"Yeah, but I like watching it on TV better. My parents won't let me have fun out on the field. They want me to be the star player or nothing."

Soccer Fan wrote his name several more times, experimenting with different morphs: printing and scripts. The one he liked best contained block letters, where the "O" in Soccer was replaced with a soccer ball. He decided it would be his official "Urth signature" from now on, if he ever had to sign anything, which he hoped he would.

"Can I have a snack?" Soccer Fan asked absent-mindedly, as he scribbled away. "Before we take off for Krog Pad?"

"Sure. What would you like?" Ideth said digging through her pack. "I have some delicious dried octopus and some seaweed bars."

Soccer Fan nearly gagged. Seafood and seaweed? Is *that* what they'd been eating? Gross! He hated seafood. He'd tried it a few times, at friends' houses, and couldn't imagine munching on it as a snack.

"You've enjoyed seafood several times since you arrived. Once you know how to prepare it properly, it's delicious. You'll get used to it, and eventually you might prefer it over everything else, even pancakes and sugary cereal. It's what happens when you have no other options."

Soccer Fan suddenly remembered a movie he'd seen about a man who'd gotten lost at sea in a little boat and had nothing to eat but raw fish. At first, the man had been disgusted and could barely keep it down. But as the days passed, he'd found it increasingly delicious. In fact, by the time he was rescued, he'd developed a great fondness for barracuda eyes.

"I won't eat fish eyes," Soccer Fan said, wanting to make that point perfectly clear.

Ideth agreed. "Okay, I won't try to feed you any, though some people think they're a delicacy. I'll bet

Shum likes them. At home, Krog Padders eat everything raw."

"Shum!" Soccer Fan suddenly remembered where they were headed that day and forgot all about the barracuda eyes. "Can we go to Krog Pad now?"

"That's the plan. Your Earth clothes are clean and ready to go into the buoy. You can wear your loin cloth under your wet suit today, instead of your boxers. A Nice Gal agreed to let me buy the one you're wearing, so it's yours now."

"Soccer Fan danced around the cabin in excitement. "I love paddling. I'm an expert. Today is going to be fun!"

Ideth smiled in amusement, recalling how terrified Soccer Fan had been of paddling the day before. He'd learned quickly, and she was pleased he'd had such a good experience. Not all findlings adapted right away, especially if the seas were rough their first time out.

"Then wriggle into your wetsuit and let's be off. Remember, there's some weather brewing that may come our way and we need to get to Krog Pad before it hits, or you'll find out that paddling isn't always so pleasant."

Ideth went to the door and got the attention of one of the East Ender employees, who carried their guest tub up to the deck.

"Stock our buoy and make sure it's sealed up tight," Ideth instructed him. "We don't want a leak, especially with a squall in the forecast."

When they reached the deck, the weather looked

fine, at least to Soccer Fan. But Ideth seemed distinctly nervous. She licked her finger and held it up, trying to gauge the direction of the wind, muttering something about "unseasonable weather."

"Is everything okay?" Soccer Fan asked uneasily.

Ideth frowned. "I don't know. The water might be rough. Please repeat the paddling rules to me before we get started. If you mix them up, you won't be safe."

Soccer Fan's mouth went dry. If Ideth was worried about the paddle, should he be terrified?

"If I tug once, it means I'm okay. If I tug twice, I want to surface. And if I tug three times I've seen a shark."

Ideth laughed despite her anxiety. "Good boy. I didn't realize you'd spotted a shark yesterday. My mind was too busy navigating. You kept that information close to your chest, didn't you?"

Soccer Fan nodded and picked up his mask and snorkel, ready to go. "Sharks are no big deal," he said casually, trying to act tough, though secretly he hoped he wouldn't encounter one again, at least not up close.

Ideth entered the water. "If the weather holds, we'll reach Krog Pad in time to set up camp before dark. It's time for you to meet your duppies."

"But what are they?" Soccer Fan asked as he followed her in. "You never told me. Are they like uppies?"

"No, not really. When we get to Krog Pad, I'll stay in the background, while your duppies will take center stage."

This didn't answer Soccer Fan's question, but he let

it pass. Now that they were in the ocean, he needed to focus on the paddle.

Ideth hitched up her harness and clipped it to the sealed buoy. Meanwhile, Soccer Fan put on his mask and snorkel as he bobbed up and down in the swell. He checked the seal on his mask by sucking in air through his nose. It held tight.

"Shum is a duppy, but he's not the only one," Ideth continued mysteriously, before going under. "Krog Pad Island is full of them, and we'll get a wild, traditional 'Krog Padder greeting' if we get there before they flop for the night. Just wait and see."

12

On Krog Pad Island

occer Fan stood on the shores of Krog Pad Island, amazed at the welcome he and Ideth were receiving. They hadn't crawled out onto the beach for more than thirty seconds before dozens of wildly enthusiastic Krog Padders were racing toward them from all directions.

"HAPPY BE! HAPPY BE!" they cried in joyous chorus as they surrounded the dripping visitors. "Look at she!" "Look at he!" "You and we! Happy be!"

They leapt, dove into the water, raced up and down the beach, and made so much noise that Soccer Fan found it almost impossible to hear what Ideth was saying to him.

"DON'T ENCOURAGE YOUR DUPPIES!" she shouted over the din. "IF YOU STAY CALM, THEY'LL QUIET DOWN!"

Soccer Fan tried to remain unruffled in the midst of the chaos, but when he saw Shum charging toward him from far up the beach, he threw open his arms and ran as fast as he could toward him. They fell into a heap on the sand and Shum gave him a big wet kiss on his forehead.

"FRANKIE see!" Shum all but choked, weeping with joy.

"I'm SOCCER FAN now!" Soccer Fan cried, thumping his chest proudly. "I renamed myself!"

Then he joined in the dancing and leaping with the rest of them: men, women, and children all mixed up together in a whirlwind of fevered exuberance, leaving Ideth to fend for herself.

Ideth sighed. "Well, here we are," she thought as she headed alone toward the cliffs across the hot sand, dragging the buoy behind her. It was much heavier when it was out of the water.

None of the Krog Padders would offer to help, she knew. They couldn't foresee, like she could, that leaving the buoy by the shoreline would mean losing it to the outgoing tide later. Ideth would have to move it alone. She struggled for a few minutes, huffing and puffing with the effort, before she reached the bottom of the limestone cliffs that rose in the center of the island. Once there, she unhitched the buoy and sat down for a rest.

She thought back on their paddle that day. Unlike

the day before, their progress had been slow. Strong winds tossed the waves high, and Soccer Fan had struggled to keep his snorkel clear.

"If only humans could store oxygen in their muscles like we can," she thought, "it would make life so much easier on us uppies."

Ideth looked down the beach to where Soccer Fan was leaping about with the Krog Padders. Then she glanced behind her, at the towering bluff. It was up to her to find a suitable cave to stow their supplies. The Krog Padders would steal them otherwise. They had no manners. None. Especially around food.

Ideth was an expert on caves. She'd lived in them all her life and knew exactly what she was looking for. The cave would need to be high up, well above the waterline should a storm and a syzygy come at the same time. The storm surges during such events were astonishing.

The Krog Padders were too preoccupied with having fun to do the hard work of finding and maintaining safe, permanent villages. The bluff was peppered with natural caves, but the Krog Padders hadn't built any trails to connect them with the beach. She'd have to scout one out for herself.

"Be no storm, need no trails!" the Krog Padders liked to say, grinning up at the wide blue sky as if it would always remain that way.

Ideth thought, "Ridiculous. They have no caves when they need them because they don't build them *before* they need them. So short-sighted!"

Still, there was no changing them. Goodness knows people had tried. She smiled when she thought of the missionaries. They'd forced the Krog Padders to wear full-body loincloths. The Krog Padders had discarded them the minute the missionaries had turned their backs, crying "No see now!"—running off in the opposite direction, naked and jubilant. Ideth sympathized with their preference for nudity.

She scanned the bluff, considering her options. Like all children raised on Cairntip Island, she'd been taught to climb almost as soon as she could walk. Trails made by uppies and their findlings never lasted long; they were obliterated by syzygy tides.

Just before sunset, she succeeded. The trail was a bit treacherous, she had to admit, but the cave had a perfectly situated fissure for venting the smoke from their fire, and the floor sloped away, so that any rain that came through the fissure disappeared into a chasm below. She spent the last hour of daylight transporting most of the supplies out of the heavy buoy and up the steep bluff, to their new home.

Another uppy had used the cave fairly recently. Items were lying about.

"You don't have time to organize things now," she told herself, looking around in displeasure. Ideth was a neat, orderly person and she was annoyed that the previous uppy hadn't cleaned up. "Yes, it's messy, but stop thinking about it. You can tidy up later."

Though the cave was a mess, she was pleased that the prior uppy had left glass jars and several bags of sugar. They'd come in handy later.

Ideth descended the bluff as the moons rose, picking her way back down to the beach and the buoy (which she'd locked up tight to discourage pilfering). She and Soccer Fan would sleep on the beach the first few nights while he adapted to his new surroundings. But she'd need to guard their buoy like a hawk. Doubtless Soccer Fan wouldn't be around to help. Once children with the gift of *Fantasy* met their duppies, there was no separating them.

She made their campsite up against the cliff. They'd have very little shelter there, but they'd have the ducky sacks, a cooking pot and spoon, and shellfish from the tide pools. She'd also retained a few luxuries in the buoy—spices, butter, oil, and such. There would be no feasting, but the supplies would get them through.

Her tummy rumbled. It was time for dinner and she needed to find Soccer Fan.

Ideth walked along the base of the cliff, keeping her eye on their campsite the whole time. As she'd anticipated, she found Soccer Fan sitting, confused, in the middle of a circle of snoring Krog Padders. He was shaking Shum, who was practically comatose, his tongue hanging out of his mouth, his legs splayed.

Seeing Ideth, Soccer Fan ran over to her. "They ate

a bunch of shellfish and then they just fell over. They haven't moved since."

"It's no use trying to wake up your duppies. They'll be sleeping like that for hours."

She reached for Soccer Fan's hand. "Let's go snug up for the night, findling. You can play with the Krog Padders again tomorrow."

The sun had dipped below the western horizon, but the moons-light was getting bright, and Ideth took the opportunity to tell Frankie a bit more about Urth's moons.

"Lunera is rocky, like your moon," she explained as they picked their way along the shoreline, heading back to the buoy. "But Ru is mostly iron and metal, like a meteorite, and though it looks smaller in the sky, it's actually more massive. Lunera is the closer of the two, but I suspect you already guessed that."

Soccer Fan knew little about moon phases. Back home, in Monterey, the canopy of trees in his neighborhood made it difficult to see the moon, much less keep track of it.

"What are we going to do here on Krog Pad?" Soccer Fan asked curiously, when they arrived at camp. "I've read stories about kids who have adventures, and watched movies about them on TV. They always learn a martial art or how to us a saber. Or kickboxing. That would be awesome!"

"Maybe." Ideth sat down on her ducky sack, crossed

her skinny legs, and leaned over to light the campfire with some matches she had on hand. "I really have no idea what will happen. My job is to get you here and take care of you as best I can. Keep you from drowning and so forth. And, of course, enjoy that wonderful imagination of yours. That's my favorite part."

Soccer Fan joined Ideth, sitting down beside her.

"You're the only one who likes my fantasies. Back home, they get me into trouble. A *lot* of trouble. All the time."

"I know," she said, striking a match. "Sometimes parents are clueless. They don't appreciate the kids they get and try to twist them into other people. But here on Krog Pad, it won't be a problem. I think your fantasy life is a riot, and your duppies will love it, too. They live in the present moment, up in their heads. You'll find you have a lot in common with them."

Soccer Fan already knew this. He'd spent three hours with Shum and his friends already, and they'd whipped up some amazing games. Sand Wars was one of his favorites. The Krog Padders split up into two groups and pretended they were warring factions, fighting for control of the island. They scooped up handfuls of wet sand and threw them at one another. When a person was hit, they had to join the opposing side, until one side won out and they all raced into the ocean to body surf.

Soccer Fan wanted to sleep with his duppies, but

Ideth discouraged it.

"You've renamed yourself so you're free to leave any-time. I'm not holding you prisoner. But I think you'll prefer to eat dinner with me. No raw seafood and rub-bery seaweed in *my* camp. Not with a nice campfire and my cooking pots."

Soccer Fan didn't need much convincing.

Ideth cracked open some oysters and asked, "Would you like them with pot nut butter or spaghetti willow oil? I prefer the oil myself, fresh pressed. Laup hap-pened to have a small bottle on hand and he popped it in with our breakfast leftovers. So thoughtful of him."

Soccer Fan was skeptical. Oysters? But he sat down, prepared to nibble at them at least.

"Back home, my parents don't let Alex and me have butter very often. They say it's bad for us. They cook with olive oil instead."

Ideth grinned. "Butter it is then. But just to warn you, it's not made from a nut. Pot nut butter comes from the ground-up pellets of Amdar pot nut owls. After the rodent bones have been removed, of course. Wouldn't want to choke."

Soccer Fan was appalled and quickly changed his mind. "Ugh! No butter for me!"

"Pot nut butter is popular here, but spaghetti willow oil is delicious too. Some people say it's addictive, and you know, I half believe it."

Soccer Fan asked cautiously, "It's made from a

plant, right?" He'd been duped into thinking that pot nut butter came from a nut. He didn't want to make that mistake again.

"Yes, and a beautiful one. Spaghetti willows are graceful, delicate trees, native to Wannabe Island. The oil harvesters have to be careful to tap only a few of the trees at a time because there aren't very many of them. That's why the oil is so expensive."

"I want to try it," said Soccer Fan. "Sounds yummy."

"All right then. But you must promise. Swear up one side and down the other. *Never* share it with the Krog Padders. They'll kick up a real fuss if they know we have it. There's nothing more annoying than a hungry Krog Padder."

Soccer Fan grinned. "Or a hungry uppy!"

"You're right," replied Ideth with a laugh, giving Soccer Fan a friendly shove. "Or a hungry findling!"

13

Marooned

occer Fan saw very little of Ideth during the first week. The weather was delightful. He played with Shum and his other exuberant duppies all day and scooted back to Ideth's camp for lunch and dinner. Sleeping out in the open, under the shadow of the towering bluffs, was pleasant. The early evenings were moons-less now, and he was able to get to sleep when it was still dark, and stay asleep until sunrise. A couple of times, after midnight, he had to get up to pee. When he did, the bright moonslight disturbed his circadian rhythm. He had to pull his ducky sack all the way over his head to get back to sleep.

He'd noticed that Lunera-shadows and Ru-shadows, by themselves, were sharp and crisp. But when both moons were up, shining from different directions, the shadows overlapped. Moons-shadows were oddly fuzzy and made it weirdly challenging to see where you were going.

On the eighth day, Ideth changed course. She'd been able to get the cave comfy and shipshape, stocked with plenty of firewood, fresh water, and enough shellfish and crabs to make seafood chowder, one of her favorite dishes. She was tired of sleeping on the beach and eating anemic meals. It was time to move.

That morning, when she fed Soccer Fan his breakfast, she laid out her plans.

"I've prepared us a comfortable cave," she said, pointing high up the bluffs. "We'll have acorn pancakes and hot win-nin up there in a couple of nights. What do you say? Win-nin nuts grow topside on this island, in abundance. When they're roasted properly, they last forever and taste like chocolate."

Soccer Fan was enthusiastic. "I'm ready for new food too, and I'm a really good climber."

In truth, Soccer Fan had climbed at the Just Hangin' Out Rock Gym in Monterey exactly once and had barely made it up the beginner's wall because he was so afraid of heights. As soon as he he'd gotten a dozen or so feet off the ground, he'd felt dizzy and sick to his stomach. He remembered it differently now. He was sure he was an experienced climber and needed no special training.

"I want you to spend the next two days practicing your climbing skills before we head up," Ideth said. "I'll help. Give you lots of tips. Climbing the bluffs,

especially for the first time, will be scary. You'll really
have to watch your step. No ropes, you see. You could
take some nasty spills and hurt yourself badly if you're
not careful."

Soccer Fan shrugged off her concerns. "I can do it.
Piece of cake."

He imagined himself zig-zagging up the bluff at
high speed, astonishing overly cautious Ideth with his
prowess.

"I don't need to practice," he added confidently.
"Let's go today. Hot win-nin sounds great."

Ideth wasn't pleased about it, but she finally agreed.
Her findling was renamed, and he could make his own
decisions, even if they were bad ones. Gathering the rest
of their belongings and organizing them in her pack,
she reluctantly showed him the way to the bottom of her
trail and they got started.

At first, Soccer Fan led the way, taking pride in leaving Ideth far behind. The trail was mostly flat at first,
and his acrophobia didn't kick in. But as the terrain
grew steep, he slowed. He had a hard time following the
narrow, pebbly path, and his heart raced. His mouth
went dry. A quarter of the way up the side of the bluff,
Ideth caught up with him.

"You're doing well, findling," she said encouragingly.
"Keep it up."

He took off again, but halfway up the bluff, he refused
to go any farther. Ideth had been right. The precipitous

terrain was terrifying. Falling to his death was now a real possibility. He was scared.

"Why do we need to come all the way up here?" he complained. "Why can't we use one of the caves lower down?"

"Not safe," Ideth replied. "Believe me, I know what I'm talking about. When our moons and sun align at syzygies, the tides rise high. If there's a storm at the same time, well, you'd better watch out. I can paddle my way through such things. I'm an Urth woman after all. But you? Not a chance. You'd drown in a heartbeat."

"I'm going back down," he announced defiantly, his knees shaking.

Ideth shrugged. "The pancakes and hot win-nin will be waiting for you. You can choose to join me or not. I'll leave little rock cairns along the way, and if you follow those, you'll end up in the right spot."

Soccer Fan was appalled. She was going to leave him behind?

"You're mean!" he snapped angrily.

"Perhaps so, but I'm also practical. I can't make your decision for you. You're a renamed child. But I've made mine."

"But it's too steep!" he cried. "And these stupid East Ender sandals don't grip the rock."

"I suggest you climb without the sandals. It might hurt a bit at first, but it's safer. Your feet will toughen up over time, just like mine."

Soccer Fan sat down beside a large boulder, clinging to it for support, refusing to budge. He didn't believe that Ideth would really leave him sitting there, alone. But she did. After handing him a flask of water, she continued her way up.

Outraged, Soccer Fan watched her go.

His face flushed red and he shouted, "My *real* parents wouldn't abandon me!" But his voice was lost to the wind.

From his aerie vantage point, he scrutinized the beach far below. The view made him woozy. He could see a few of the Krog Padders out and about, tiny ants from his lofty perspective. He longed to be with them, on the flat beach.

He told himself, "I don't need old Ideth and her stupid cave. I don't care if I have to eat raw seafood. I'm going back to my duppies."

He didn't really mean it. He *would* mind eating raw seafood. However, in that moment he convinced himself it wouldn't be half bad.

He stood up and tried to pick his way back down the cliff, but it was devilishly hard to keep his footing. Going down, it turned out, was even scarier than going up. He kept losing his balance, landing hard on his butt. He paused to get his bearings. Perhaps there was an easier approach.

He looked off to his right. Two boulders blocked the path, but he thought that maybe if he squeezed through them he'd have better luck.

He slipped through the slender notch and picked his way straight ahead. After a short distance, he saw a possible opening, a gap.

Up close, though, the narrow fissure, a steep chute, disappeared into empty air. He looked upward to where the chute apparently began, high above. It offered a direct route from the top of the bluff down to the beach, but it was much too steep to navigate safely. His heart hammered in his chest, his fear of heights taking over. He felt nauseated and woozy. He was sure he'd pitch forward and fall into the yawning mouth of the fissure if he stayed in his present position one more moment.

Discouraged, he decided to retrace his steps and go back to where Ideth had left him. He'd climbed her trail once. Maybe he could navigate his way down it, if he kept his wits about him.

It was a wise plan, but when he turned around, he couldn't figure out where the two large boulders were. He'd lost his landmarks. There were dozens of boulders, and they all looked the same from this new angle.

They all looked the same.

A chill swept over him. Where was their trail? Which way had they come up? He felt the wind lift his hair.

Soccer Fan peered up the cliff, looking for cairns. But despite looking very hard, he didn't see any. Not one. He was off course.

He fumed. "How could she do this to me? I'll never find a way out of this mess."

He eased himself to the ground with a feeling of impending doom. But as he dug his foot into the soil and kicked some of it downhill in frustration, he suddenly remembered something that eased his fear and made him smile.

Ideth wasn't serious, of course. She was playing a game with him, the same game his parents played all the time with him back home. They'd get all tough, threatening to make him "live with the consequences" of his actions, but they always rescued him. Just last month, he'd forgotten a permission slip for a field trip, and when his mother had dropped him off at school, she'd been angry.

"This is what happens when you don't take responsibility," she'd chided him in an ominous tone. "Your teacher is going to make you stay behind while the others are out having fun."

But by the time the bus drew up, prepared to whisk the kids off to the Monterey Bay Aquarium, his permission slip had magically made its way to his teacher. His mother had driven home to get it.

"Ideth will be back," Soccer Fan told himself smugly. Then he said aloud, in a mocking tone: "Am I right, or am I right?"

He was wrong.

While Soccer Fan sat in the hot sun on the side of the cliff, waiting for Ideth to climb back down and save him, Ideth was busy gathering win-nin nuts in preparation for dinner. She had no intention of rescuing Soccer Fan. The idea never entered her mind.

"I'd forgotten how big the nuts grow here," she thought, inhaling the heavenly fumes up her nostrils as she cracked one open with her teeth.

She filled her backpack with the golden nuts.

Meanwhile, Soccer Fan was having a lovely time, too, exploring the ground beneath his feet, whiling away the hours watching some busy ants remove a twig from the entrance to their hole. He imagined himself to be one of them. Did ants sleep? Did they dream? Every now and then he switched roles and used a stick to make their task easier, a benevolent God helping from above. After a while, he'd given the ants names. Ghost was bone white, unlike the others, who were jet black. He seemed to be the boss. Teeny was tiny but very strong. She was the most industrious of the lot. Scout never followed the main trail. He went off on his own, looking for new sources of food.

Soccer Fan had a great time, and he could have played "Ant City" for days on end. But as evening settled in, an uneasy feeling settled over him. The sun was low in the sky, he suddenly realized, and Ideth was nowhere in sight.

The cliffside was quiet and still. A late afternoon lull. He stood up and scanned the cliffs above, hoping to see Ideth making her way down. When he didn't, he yelled her name, several times. Maybe she was out looking for him and needed some help. After all, he wasn't where she'd expect him to be.

No reply.

A flash of movement caught his eye. A lizard peeked out from behind a nearby rock.

She's not coming, buddy! it seemed to say when he looked at it. *You're on your own!*

Soccer Fan's heart dropped. He couldn't believe it. Could the lizard be right? Suddenly, he was dead certain it was.

Ideth wouldn't be coming to rescue him. He'd be spending the night on the side of the bluff alone. No dinner. No ducky sack. No moons until much later. He couldn't go down safely, and he didn't dare go up. *He was marooned!*

It took a moment for the truth to sink in. Then his eyes filled with hot tears. He hated crying, but he couldn't help himself. One tear spilled out of the corner of his right eye and wound its way down his cheek.

Unlike the Frankie with the aunts and the goats, who lived in a culture where boys were allowed to cry without judgment (lucky him), Soccer Fan thought crying was a sign of weakness. Whenever he felt like crying, he retreated into his imagination, where he could distract himself quickly to escape the pain. But fantasizing wasn't going to help him out of his current predicament. He'd have to make a nest behind a boulder and hope it didn't budge from his weight and send him cascading down the cliff. What if there was a rockfall in the night? Did nasty creatures, like bluff spiders, come out after dark? They were probably huge with seventeen eyes apiece and razor-sharp teeth. Going down wasn't an option. He'd already tried that. Descending was even more scary than going up.

Soccer Fan angrily wiped away the unwanted tear. "Stupid Ideth!" he thought. "This sucks! I'll have to go up!"

The sun disappeared behind a layer of shifting clouds and then slipped out the other side. Temporarily blinded, Soccer Fan shaded his eyes so he could see better. High on his perch above the clouds, he looked out to sea, hoping, one last time, for rescue. Perhaps a helicopter would come roaring up from the beach below and five friendly paramedics would hop out, delighted to see him. In the blink of an eye, they'd whisk him off to Ideth's cave and carry him inside. Ha! Wouldn't *that* surprise her?

But alas, all Soccer Fan saw was a vast expanse of endless blue. So, with no other choice, he let his fantasy go and returned his attention to the task at hand, cautiously picking his way back in the general direction from which he'd come. He needed to find the spot where he and Ideth had parted ways. That was his only hope of finding her trail.

After about ten minutes of searching, he spied a low, scrubby tree that looked familiar. Then he saw his water flask, sitting beside it. He'd left it there by accident, and

*High on his perch above the clouds, Soccer Fan looked
out to sea, hoping, one last time, for rescue...*

was glad that he had. What a relief! It was a beacon
of hope in the frightening wilderness that kept changing on him as he moved, leaving him disoriented and
unsure if he was going the right way.

He picked up the flask, took a swig of water (he was
parched) and looked up the bluff, scanning for cairns.
It took him a minute, but finally he thought he spied
one. Trembling, he navigated the crumbly, hazardous "use trail" toward it, his legs scissoring with fear.
When he reached it and saw that Ideth had arranged
some rocks beside the cairn to make a "happy face," he
couldn't help but smile, despite the adrenalin coursing
through his veins.

Resting for a moment, too frightened to look down, he scanned the bluff above him again and saw another cairn, and another after that, marking a trail that climbed steeply, with no switchbacks, into the rocks high above.

It took him more than an hour, and he had to stop often to catch his breath. The shadows lengthened ominously, and he was sure he'd never reach the end of the trail before nightfall. But the idea of hot win-nin by a campfire sharpened his focus. Finally, after what seemed like a hellish eternity, he spied the mouth to Ideth's cave. And none too soon, for the sun was sitting on the horizon.

A Krog Pad willow broom marked the opening.

When Soccer Fan reached the cave and looked within, Ideth was busy puttering about. She looked up when he said a weary "hello" and smiled, seemingly oblivious to what he'd just endured.

"Ah ha! There you are," she cried brightly. "Come on in, snuggle up by the fire, and grab a plate. Acorn pancakes are divine and you got here just in time to get them sizzling hot, straight off the pan."

"And hot win-nin too, right?" he asked, entering the cave.

"As promised," Ideth said passing him a cup of the steaming liquid.

When dinner was over, Ideth cleaned up the dishes, throwing Soccer Fan a dishtowel to help dry. After his awful afternoon, Soccer Fan took it without thinking. Drying dishes was nothing compared to his experience on the bluff. He was vastly relieved to be under Ideth's protection again, on flat ground, and he figured that if it meant chipping in now and then, oh, well.

After they'd cleaned up, Ideth read Soccer Fan a story from one of her books, *Tales by Moons-light: Stories from before the Great Melt*. It was about a wicked man named Rune Oft who called himself an "astrovisionary," and the prince who exposed him as a fraud. Soccer Fan found himself caught up in the tale, enjoying the last vestiges of the evening fire as the flames died away, replaced by glowing embers.

"Time to turn in," Ideth yawned, as she put the book away. "Perhaps we can go cliff diving in the morning. Any boy who can climb a steep bluff with the courage you did this afternoon would surely be up for it."

Soccer Fan knew she was kidding. He could see the twinkle in her eye.

"No way! I'd miss the water and crack open my head!" he replied. "I almost did today, thanks to you."

"If you'd practiced for a couple days in advance, it would have been easier. It pays to plan ahead now and then, don't you think?"

Ideth was right, of course. Soccer Fan knew it, but he wasn't going to admit it.

Instead, he grumbled, "Ugh. Whatever. I never want to climb that bluff again."

"Well, if you want to play with your duppies, you're going to have to get over your fear. They're down there, and we're up here, aren't we?"

Soccer Fan gulped. He hadn't thought of that.

14

A Break in the Case

Yup! Yup! We've arrested someone," Officer Morgan reported to Frankie's parents. He was standing in their living room, looking triumphant.

"Oh, thank goodness," Frankie's mother whispered, slumping against her husband.

Three weeks had passed since Frankie went missing, and there hadn't been any leads. Now that the police had arrested someone, maybe they'd find out where Frankie was. Maybe they'd get him back at last.

"The suspect's denying any involvement," Officer Morgan continued. "But remember that bloody dish towel we found in your kitchen? We thought it was Frankie's blood? Well, it turns out we were wrong. The crime lab tested it for DNA and it belongs to a roofer named Jimmy Albini. His DNA profile's in the national

CODIS database because he committed another crime, you see. It was easy for the lab to identify him."

"What's CODIS?" Evelyn asked.

"Big collection of DNA profiles from criminals. Very helpful when tracking down killers."

Killers.

"You mean..." she continued.

Before she could say any more, Officer Morgan's cell phone began ringing the theme to Star Wars, and he held up a finger to silence her while he took the call.

"Yup, yup! I see," he said, as he listened to the person on the other end of the line. "Well, what did they do with the body then? Is it in the morgue?"

"Is Frankie dead?" asked Roberto, stepping in front of his wife to protect her from the news.

Evelyn breathed in sharply, her hand over her mouth. She'd been dreading this moment. If Frankie was dead, she didn't know how she'd go on living. She'd have to, for Alex, but it would be terrible.

"Another case," Officer Morgan mouthed at Roberto and Evelyn, to their enormous relief, before turning his attention back to his call.

He listened for another thirty seconds or so, clearly annoyed, and then barked, "Well, thanks for the update!" Then he secured the phone to a hook on his belt and turned back to face Frankie's parents, as if nothing had just happened.

"Now, where were we?" he asked, scanning his mem-

ory. "Ah, yes. I was just about to tell you that we don't know where Frankie is, but we're hoping the suspect will tell us. Yup, yup! I can't make any promises, but we'll try to get to the bottom of what happened. Dead or alive, we'll do everything we can to find your son. At least we have a lead now. This late in the game, we often never find out what happened. Cases grow cold and we have to move on. Sad but true."

He pulled out a pad of paper and began scribbling.

"Grocery list," he smiled apologetically. "If I don't write things down when they enter my mind, I forget about them. Drives my wife crazy."

Roberto and Evelyn looked at each other, their eyebrows furrowed in anger. Officer Morgan was making a *grocery list* while their son was missing and might still be alive awaiting rescue? How could he be so relaxed at a time like this? They wanted him to act!

"I remember Jimmy," Evelyn said, trying to move the investigation forward. "He works for Bob's Roofing. But I don't think he's the right guy. He's such a nice man! So polite. He was the only one who could find the hole in the roof above Frankie's bedroom. We hired him to patch it, but then Frankie went missing, and we called him off the job."

Officer Morgan nodded grimly. "It often happens that way. Yup! The man comes to work at the home. Sees the kid is all alone. Snatches him. Crime of opportunity. Then the child is dead within a matter of hours.

These criminals like to cover their tracks. Usually get rid of the body down a mineshaft or some such. If we're lucky, we might find Frankie's bones."

Evelyn dissolved into tears.

"Enough!" Roberto snapped. "I appreciate you keeping us informed, Officer Morgan, but I will *not* have you upsetting my wife. She's not up to this. You're the most insensitive person I've ever met."

Officer Morgan was taken aback. He thought he was being helpful. But he could see, now, that he'd just made matters worse. He apologized and left rather abruptly, but before he went, he assured Roberto and Evelyn that he would stay in touch.

"I'll call you with more details as I get them. You'll be the first to know. Yup! Definitely before the press does, anyhow."

Frankie's parents sat down on the couch in their living room. Evelyn was shaking. The solar panels atop the fine house by the sea glinted in the sun. Mush banged his food bowl.

"At least they have a suspect," she whispered, in a resigned tone. "Surely we can't expect any other kind of good news at this point."

Later that evening, Roberto's cell phone rang and he took the call.

It was Officer Morgan with an update.

"Albini's boss just confirmed that Jimmy was working at your house on the day Frankie disappeared. And Albini's got a rap sheet that'll make you want to weep."

"We're weeping already, I can assure you," Roberto replied, coldly. He couldn't believe how blasé Officer Morgan was being about the whole affair.

"If he was a doctor," Roberto thought, "he'd tell his patient 'Yup! Yup! You're dying of heart disease! You can't expect to live much longer now. You'd better choose a tombstone!'"

There was a pause on the line and Roberto could hear the sound of someone (could it be Officer Morgan?) typing on a keyboard.

Roberto thought in dismay, "He's not even listening to me!"

It was true. Officer Morgan didn't know what to do with himself if he wasn't multi-tasking. He had to keep busy to avoid facing how disappointed he was with his life. Being a police officer wasn't at all the way he'd envisioned it when he was a boy. Back in first grade, he'd told everyone he wanted to be a cop and puffed out his tiny chest with pride. Now he wished he'd known what he was getting into. No one liked having to tell the parents of a missing child that the kid was probably dead and they might never find him, even his bones. What a terrible job he had, especially at times like this.

"Well, I just thought you should know the way the winds are blowing," Officer Morgan said, his hands poised over his keyboard in mid-sentence. He was typing up a report that was a week overdue and he needed to get it done or there'd be trouble.

"Please keep trying to find Frankie," Roberto replied. He was annoyed but did not want to alienate Officer Morgan by showing his anger and impatience. "He might still be alive, and there's no time to waste."

"Yes, I assure you I will. There's nothing as terrible as *not knowing what happened,* is there?"

Officer Morgan snapped shut his cell phone, leaving Roberto with his mouth open, hoping against hope that Frankie would be found safe and alive despite the policeman's apparent indifference.

15

Iktae

After the day on the bluffs, life fell into a happy routine for Ideth and Soccer Fan. Soccer Fan didn't attempt to descend the steep trail to the beach again, but he did wander from the cave to scout around, looking down on his tiny, distant duppies, longing to be with them. One day, during his explorations, he stumbled onto the entrance to the dizzying chute he'd seen on the day Ideth had marooned him. Peering into its yawning mouth, he felt woozy.

Over time, he forged his own trail, a much safer route with plenty of switchbacks that also offered him a brief, tantalizing view of the eastern side of the island. One day, he finally made it down to the beach, where his duppies greeted him joyously, leaping and running about feverishly, grinning from ear to ear, as if they were meeting him for the first time.

Pretty soon, he was making the journey every day, hiking downhill after breakfast and then uphill in the late afternoon, before dinner. He was careful to leave the beach with plenty of time to spare. He didn't want to get caught out on the trail after sundown. Even if there was Lunera-light, or Ru-light, or even moons-light, he didn't dare push his luck. He was still scared silly of heights, and didn't want to get into another terrifying situation.

In the mornings, Ideth woke early, puttering in her hush-hush way that made her lovable, but interfered with his sleep. He woke, fell asleep, woke again, fell asleep, woke again, fell asleep, and finally woke up for good with a sigh. Then they made breakfast together. When Ideth did the cooking, Soccer Fan cleaned up, and when Soccer Fan did the cooking, Ideth cleaned up.

Soccer Fan was no goody-two-shoes. He hadn't suddenly become a different person. Sometimes he shirked the work, but Ideth didn't seem to mind. She never nagged him about helping. She didn't give him "BLAH, BLAH, BLAH" lectures. For Soccer Fan, that made all the difference. He helped when he felt like it, which was most days because Ideth made helping fun.

Often, they goofed around. One morning, while he was drying one of her precious plates, he cried "Oops!!" and pretended to drop it. The horrified look on Ideth's face sent him into peals of laughter. When she realized he was joking, she chased him around the cave with her broom until they were both out of breath and fell to the floor, tears of mirth spilling out of their eyes.

"I was thinking maybe Shum and I could play beach Frisbee with it," Soccer Fan grinned, holding the plate just a few inches out of her reach.

"Not a chance," replied Ideth, still laughing. "My grandmother gave me those plates and if you break them I'll skin your hide."

About a month after his first scary trip up the bluff, Soccer Fan was more comfortable with climbing. The trail he'd forged for himself was easy now. He could ascend it in less than two hours, and descend it in forty-five minutes, if he pushed himself.

When he reached the beach each morning, he went to find his duppies. Then he spent the rest of the day playing wildly imaginative games with them—and reading.

Shum, it turned out, had a daughter, a wide-eyed little girl named Iktae, who was unusually shy for a Krog Padder. Somehow, she'd gotten hold of a book, which she carried around with her like a sodden doll. It was an unusual toy for a child to have on Krog Pad, an island with no schools or libraries. Soccer Fan was curious to know where she'd found it.

"Come with me!" she whispered to Soccer Fan when he asked her about it. She took him by the hand and led him to a bushy area at the foot of the bluffs. Soccer Fan could see the remains of a wrecked rowboat sticking out of the sand.

Pointing first to the boat and then back to her book, she said, "From the sea."

Soccer Fan raised his eyebrows in understanding. The book, it seemed, had been shipwrecked.

"Books good be!" Soccer Fan said, speaking in the choppy Krog Pad dialect he'd grown so fond of. "Other worlds see."

"Other worlds be?" Iktae asked, clearly confused.

Soccer Fan nodded while fingering the pages doubtfully. The book was damp and the pages were matted together. The back cover was missing altogether, as if someone had purposely ripped it off, and the binding was tattered. He flipped it over and could just make out the title: *Insurance Law: Cairntip Province.*

"I'll have to borrow *Tales by Moons-light*," he thought. "I could easily turn Iktae off of reading with a snoozer like this."

Ideth was willing to lend him the book, but not without a word of caution.

"You mustn't let the Krog Padders get it. They'll rip the book to shreds."

Soccer Fan didn't tell her that he was planning to read the book to Iktae, but Ideth knew.

"Oh dear," she thought. "I hope he doesn't get too attached to that little girl. It might not turn out well." But she didn't express her concerns to Soccer Fan.

Thus, under the bright Krog Pad sky, Iktae's reading lessons began. Every day after lunch, when the Krog

Padders flopped for an hour or so, Soccer Fan and Iktae ran off together, to the rowboat, and Soccer Fan read to her. He started with the first story, *The Moons-lings*. The heroine, a strong, clever girl named Margie, was an excellent role model for timid Iktae, who perked up when Margie solved three moons-riddles to free herself and her brother from an evil sorceress.

Iktae was entranced, and as soon as Soccer Fan finished one story, she begged him to go on. Like all Krog Padders, she had a vivid imagination and could paint pictures in her mind with ease. In fact, Soccer Fan realized, Iktae had a difficult time separating fantasy from reality. Sometimes she took on the persona of one of the characters for days at a time, and Soccer Fan had a hard time getting her to snap out of it.

"I Laly be," she might say. "I love p-siders."

P-siders were much like spiders and, according to the book, lived on Urth before the Great Melt and produced valuable silk. In *The Six Woes of Werd*, Laly's father kept a colony of them. They were ugly creatures and most people were repulsed by them. But lovely Laly gave them names and tended them with great care.

It took them a few weeks to work their way through the book because Iktae was a slow learner. Her native Krog Pad language was an abbreviated one with a limited vocabulary and excessive exclamation marks. Many of the words in the book were new to her, and when she tried to pronounce them, she stumbled. Yet, day by day, her skills improved until she was reading at Kindergarten level. Soccer Fan read aloud to her, using his finger to guide her through the passages, and soon she took over, doing the same.

Soccer Fan noticed, in particular, that the future tense was impossible for Iktae to comprehend. It seemed that the Krog Padder brain was stuck in the present and there was no cure.

"No, Iktae, it happens *later,* not right now."

She looked at him like he was a wizard.

In this respect, she was like the other Krog Padders, who played all day long, lost in whatever was happening at the time, with no eye to what was coming next. They spent their time tossing conch shells back and forth over a seaweed net, performing various acrobatic feats to impress one another, and running around in circles until they got too dizzy to stand and collapsed to the ground in glee. When they were hungry, they scooped up whatever the tides washed in. When Soccer Fan asked them what they planned to do the next day, they gave him a blank stare, as if he were talking gibberish.

Nevertheless, Iktae picked up the skill of reading, a bit at a time. She worked very hard at their "lessons," and, along the way, bonded tightly with Soccer Fan. She thought he was the most wonderful, brilliant, amazing big brother a girl could have, and she followed him around like a puppy.

"How's Iktae's reading coming along?" Ideth queried,

one evening after dinner.

"I figured you knew about it," Soccer Fan said. "We finished *Tales by Moons-light* this morning. She read the last chapter on her own, from beginning to end. The one about the kingdom and queendom that were at war for a thousand years."

Ideth sighed happily, relieved they were done with the book and that she'd be getting it back in one piece. "Oh good. That book is one of my favorites, and it's a first edition, you know."

There was a silence, followed by another silence, and then a third, even longer one.

A pot nut owl let out a hoot in the distance. A sliver of crescent Ru-light darted into the cave, as the moon made its way to the western horizon, following the sun.

"I'm really, really sorry, Ideth," Soccer Fan finally said with an embarrassed grimace. "Shum got it. There was nothing I could do."

Ideth heaved an exasperated sigh. She'd been afraid of this. The last time she'd been on the island, one of the Krog Padders had gotten into her buoy before she'd been able to get her supplies safely to a cave. They'd stolen all her food, and her books had been torn to shreds. Krog Padders loved to chew on anything they could get their hands on. Books were irresistible to them. "Not that they even try to control themselves," she stewed. "They just do whatever makes them happy without giving any thought to others. So self-centered."

"Did he destroy the whole thing?"

"Yeah, sorry. Iktae's the only one who respects books. But Shum had so much fun doing it that I had a hard time being angry."

Ideth replied in annoyance, "Humph. That's typical. But it's such a shame. I love the story where the girl uses her wits to escape the clutches of her wicked grandfather."

"Me too. Along the way, I could see how she was going to do it. But Iktae didn't understand what was happening until the very end. She can't see the future."

Ideth smiled. She wanted to say, "You couldn't do it very well either, before you got out from under those suffocating parents of yours."

Instead, she said, "It certainly is. I've never known a Krog Padder who could look ahead. They're not built for it."

"When I say things like 'Ru will come back,' and 'When the tide goes out,' she shrugs it off. She has no idea what I'm talking about. Maybe I can teach her to be different."

Soccer Fan imagined himself to be a brilliant professor, winning the award for "Best Teacher on Urth." His academic robe would be bright red, he decided, and his cap would be ink black with a tassel made of real gold.

Ideth grinned. "That black robe of yours is very handsome, though I prefer bright orange myself. Sets off the color of my skin, or so one of my uppy colleagues tells me. But I'm afraid you'd be barking up the wrong

tree with Iktae. She's stuck in the here and now. She can remember the past when she puts her mind to it, but the future is another thing altogether."

Soccer Fan thought about what Ideth was telling him. He wasn't sure that Iktae's fate was sealed. Perhaps she could get a glimmer of the future someday. After all, she'd learned to read, hadn't she? This already set her apart from the others.

"Did you know that Iktae's already renamed herself?" he asked.

"Yes, I know. All the children on this island rename themselves early."

"But why? I asked her about it, but she doesn't have a clue. Ideas like 'early' and 'late' don't mean anything to her."

"I'm not sure. The Krog Padders have their own ways, I suppose."

A shadow fell across Ideth's face, and Soccer Fan sensed that she was hiding something. Ideth was an upbeat kind of person, but she was obviously unsettled now. He peppered Ideth with questions, but the more he pushed, the quieter she became. Soon, she made an excuse to turn in early, promising scallop burgers the next day, knowing they were Soccer Fan's favorite. Frustrated, Soccer Fan wished he had the gift of *Reading Minds*. He wanted to know what was bothering her.

Soccer Fan dreamed about Iktae that night, as he often did those days. Usually, their romps together were fun, and he woke up rested and in a good mood. But this time, his dreams were oddly off-kilter. As the hours wore on, he restlessly slipped in and out of consciousness. Iktae's dream face, huge and out of focus, merged with Shum's face, then Ideth's, then his mother's, then Mush's. All of them stared at him with forlorn, pleading eyes.

Just before dawn, he woke with a start. A little hole had opened up inside of him, deep down inside, where fear comes from, and he lay in the near-dark, his heart banging.

When Ideth started her puttering a few minutes later, he got dressed and left the cave, grabbing a slice of bluff berry pie on the way out. Quickly, he made his way down to the beach, intent on checking on Iktae, to make sure she was okay.

She was, and Soccer Fan relaxed, shrugging off his anxiety. He wasn't the kind of kid to brood, and once he knew that his fears were unfounded, he forgot about his nightmare.

He thought, "Sometimes you just have a bad night. No big deal." Then he followed Iktae out to the surf, where they spent the day imagining they were carrier gulls ferrying messages between an imprisoned princess and the boy she loved, while Shum and the rest pretended they were flying whales.

16

Neap Tides

My duppies are hungry!" shouted Soccer Fan, running into the cave, where Ideth was mending his pier diving suit.

Ideth looked up. Soccer Fan was tanned and fit in his loincloth. His feet were tough with callouses. His easy confidence was unmistakable.

She didn't seem surprised that the Krog Padders were hungry. Looking up from her work she said, "Of course they are. The neap tides have come."

Soccer Fan frowned. "What do you mean?"

"The pulls of Lunera, Ru, and the sun have evened out. The tides will stand still for a few days. No tides bringing the food in. No tides taking the water out."

"But what will they eat if they can't go beachcombing?"

"Nothing much," she replied, matter-of-factly.

Soccer Fan was appalled. These were his friends,

Shum's people. His duppies. He couldn't let them go hungry, especially little Iktae.

"They're moping about on the beach crying 'Poor we! Hungry be! No food! No food see!' I've never seen them like this. It's horrible!"

Ideth pursed her lips. "Ha! Well, it serves them right. They don't harvest more food than they need when the pickings are abundant. They just leave the leftovers and let the tides take them away. Now they have nothing saved up and I'm supposed to feel sorry for them? I don't think so. They made their own bed, now they can lie in it."

Soccer Fan felt like stamping his foot, but he restrained himself. He knew that anger would only get in his way.

"Well, I don't care what you say. There must be something we can do to help them. We have extra food, a whole cave full of it. You've been bottling up bluff berry jam, roasting win-nin berries, and grinding acorn flour for weeks. Can't we share some of it, just to get them through?"

Ideth turned her head and looked directly into his eyes, one brow raised.

"Seems to me that the Krog Padders are responsible for themselves. If you feed them, you're just enabling them to remain the way they are. I know it seems harsh, but that's how it is. They'll not be getting any of my food and, fortunately, they can't raid my stocks because they can't climb up here."

Soccer Fan was defiant. "I've renamed myself. I can take them food if I want."

"Not true," Ideth informed him. "You can't steal other people's belongings and get away with it. You can't become an outlaw. I'm the one who made the jam, and I'm the one who picked and dried the win-nin nuts and acorns. It's my food, and they're not getting any."

Soccer Fan slumped to the floor by the mouth of the cave.

"I can't stand watching them. I had a conch burger in my pocket and they could smell it. They stood around me in a circle, with their eyes fixed on it. I tore it up into small pieces and shared it around, but no one got very much. When I started back for the cliff, they followed me howling: 'Soccer Fan see! We no happy be! Give food we!'"

Soccer Fan looked out over the lip of the cave to the beach below. He couldn't quite see the Krog Padders because they were huddled at the bottom of the trail, where he'd left them. But he could hear their wails over the gentle slosh of the distant surf.

Ideth was disgusted. "Big bunch of overgrown babies. They'll go hungry for a few days and then they'll forget all about it. As soon as the tides shift, they'll get busy eating again and start shouting 'Happy be!' You just wait and see."

Soccer Fan retreated deeper into the cave to escape from the wails of the Krog Padders. He didn't think he'd be able to eat while they went hungry. He couldn't understand how Ideth could just sit there, slurping up jam, when she knew what was happening on the beach. "I'll go on a hunger strike," he thought. "That will change Ideth's mind."

Soccer Fan started his hunger strike immediately after lunch. (If you ever decide to go on a hunger strike, you'll find that it's easier to start right after a big meal.) Then he broke the strike for dinner because Ideth made scallop burgers fried in a smidgen of spaghetti willow oil, too delicious to resist.

We must give Soccer Fan some much-deserved credit here, for he managed to skip both breakfast and lunch the following day without sneaking anything behind Ideth's back. But by dinnertime, he'd lost his willpower and was beginning to side with her about the whole affair.

"I guess a little fast won't hurt them, if it lasts only a few days. Are you sure the tides will return soon? I miss my duppies."

"Like clockwork," she promised. "You'll see. For the time being, though, you'd better stay up here, out of the fray."

Soccer Fan hatched a plan. Shum and his like could suffer for a few days, he decided, but he wasn't going to let it happen to Iktae. It wasn't her fault her people didn't prepare for the neaps.

"Show me how to make jam," Soccer Fan said. "If I make my own stock, I can do what I want with it, right?"

"That's true," Ideth said. "And it's not hard. We'll go topside and gather some berries today."

There was an easy route to the top of the bluff with no scary exposure, and Soccer Fan enjoyed his time on its flat surface. It was crazy-windy, but the view was spectacular. He could see some islands in the distance, and he wondered about them. Did they have Finding Fruit like Finding Island? Or perhaps they hosted species of bizarre flying tigers or pink rats with green eyes. Wouldn't that be something?

Over the ensuing two hours, Soccer Fan learned that gathering bluff berries was a bit of an art. You had to avoid the sharp, prickly spines on the stems. Ideth showed him how to manage without getting stabbed in the fingers, and after a few painful "lessons," he got it right.

Once back in the cave, Ideth walked him through the next steps.

"Pour the berries into the pot and add about four cups of water and two cups of sugar. Then boil them up good 'til the jam is clinging to the spoon. After that, scoop it into the bottles and seal the lids down tight. Once the bottles are cool to the touch, you're done."

Soccer Fan did as Ideth directed, and when the batch was ready to taste, he found that his jam was just as good as hers: smooth and yummy as could be.

"I'm going to take a jar down to Iktae," he thought, "but I need to do it at night. Otherwise the Krog Padders might see me. I don't want that. They'd take the jam right off me, no apologies."

After a dinner of dried octopus with lime sauce (which was a bit rubbery), Soccer Fan curled up with Ideth's second book, a cooking guide titled *The Good Urth*, biding his time. Ru was full, so he'd have some moonlight for his journey, but Lunera was a slender waxing crescent and would follow the sun over the lip of the western horizon soon after sunset. He wished he dared take Ideth's hurricane lantern with him, but he knew he couldn't make it down the bluff safely if he was carrying it in one hand. He was a moderately good climber now, but even on his relatively safe, switchbacked trail, he still needed all his appendages to manage.

The Good Urth was a cookbook with recipes from nearly every island on the planet: Cairntip Deep Dish Salmon Potato Pie, Grilled Amdar Halibut with Chilled Lemon Hazelnut Sauce, Spicy Wannabe Shrimp and Conch Pasta.

Recipes native to Krog Pad Island and Finding Island, however, were notably absent.

"There is no culinary culture on Krog Pad Island," the author wrote, dismissively. For Finding Island, she referred her readers to a companion book: *Surviving a Finding: Fruit, Fruit, and More Fruit*, calling it "the definitive work on the topic."

Of particular interest was a chapter called "Persevering through Preserving." It included detailed instructions on how to preserve food so it would last a long time. Sub-chapters included Drying, Fermenting, Canning, and Chemical Treatment. If he could teach Iktae the basics, and latch her onto the idea, she'd never go hungry during the neap tides again.

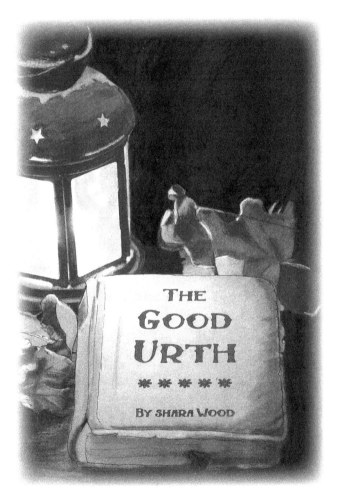

The Good Urth was a cookbook with recipes from nearly every island on the planet...

About nine p.m., he made his move. Borrowing Ideth's pack, he popped a jar of jam inside, left the cave, and started down.

It was very challenging to see where he was going under the dim, orange Ru-light. Fortunately, he knew the route practically by heart. Keeping an eye out for landmarks, he stayed on course. Twice he got lost and had to backtrack, but he finally reached the beach.

Soccer Fan knew where his duppies would be flopped. They usually slept in the same place, tucked up against the bluff, where there was little wind.

He was familiar with each one now—there were sixty-two in all. When he'd first arrived on Krog Pad, they'd all looked pretty much alike, but when he'd spent more time with them, he'd picked up on subtle differences.

Soccer Fan was familiar with this phenomenon. Back home in Monterey, a few years before, his parents had started taking him to the new zoo. At first, all the lions had looked alike. But pretty soon he was calling the female one with the short tail Sally and the male one with the black mane Simba.

Moving toward the duppies, he reached Dubdy first. Dubdy had an extra finger on his left hand and was the fastest paddler among them. He was curled in a tight ball, sleeping through his misery. Then Soccer Fan stumbled on Saidy, who was plumper than the others. Her unusually roomy nose was wiggling and her eyelids were twitching. She was dreaming about food, for sure.

Soccer Fan wandered through the sleeping forms until he found Iktae, lying beside Shum. Her mother, Dyla, was on the other side, a protective arm resting across her daughter's back.

"I need to get her away from everyone before I try to wake her," he thought. "If I alert any of the others, they'll see I have food. It's not even worth contemplating what *that* would be like."

Soccer Fan gently shifted Iktae's sleeping body so he could slide her out from between her parents. Then he carried her out to the rowboat.

"Wake up, Iktae," he whispered. "I have bluff berry jam!"

Iktae remained limp in his arms. "Food!" he whispered again, a little louder, shaking her gently.

This time she heard him, and her quiet, shy eyes opened. "I made the jam myself," he told her proudly. "Just for you."

Iktae sat up slowly, for she was quite weak from hunger, but when Soccer Fan retrieved the jar from Ideth's backpack and opened the lid, she became excited. The fragrance of the jam quickly diffused into the air, wafting up her nose.

"You prince be!" she cried softly, sitting up, fully awake now, her eyes alight.

Soccer Fan unscrewed the lid and handed Iktae the spoon he'd brought along. As he watched her scoop up the jam, he felt a mixture of pride and joy. She was obviously very hungry. She finished off the entire jar in a jiffy.

When she was done, Soccer Fan said, "You mustn't tell anyone else about this or there'll be trouble. It's only a few more days until the tides return, but I'll come down from the bluffs every night to feed you. I won't come down during the day, though. The others won't leave me alone if I do."

Iktae nodded solemnly.

"It's all about looking ahead," Soccer Fan said. "If you plan for the neap tides, you can get ready for them and no one needs to go hungry."

Soccer Fan packed away the empty jar and cinched his pack. Then he walked Iktae back to her sleeping parents. As she lay down, he whispered in her ear, "Remember, I'll come down every night, around this time." Then he left her.

Frankie's nighttime trips were hazardous. Even though Lunera-light returned as the nights passed, joining a waning gibbous Ru, the fuzzy moons-shadows threw him off. He slipped several times, giving himself some nasty scrapes. But he was faithful to Iktae. He brought her jam every night, despite some bloody knees.

Slowly the tides returned. Then one morning, when Soccer Fan looked down from the cave, he saw that life on Krog Pad Island was back to normal. Shum and his buddies were running joyously up and down the beach, leaping in the waves. That night, Soccer Fan got his first decent night's sleep in four days.

As he and Ideth crawled into their ducky sacks, she turned to him.

In the near-dark, she said, "Well done, findling. It's not easy to climb in moons-shadows. I know. I nearly fell to my death one night on this very same bluff, years ago."

"Well, I couldn't let her go hungry," Soccer Fan said.

Suddenly, an image of Mush materialized in his head. The dog's big black eyes stared at him, mournfully, through the patio door. He banged his dish with his paw. No one came to feed him.

"Good looking puppy," Ideth said.

"You know, Mush reminds me of a Krog Padder," Soccer Fan said. "If my parents didn't feed him, he'd go hungry, just like them."

"Lucky he has your parents, then," Ideth replied.

Soccer Fan freely admitted that he was the one who was supposed to feed Mush. "It's my only chore," he explained.

"Chore? Why is it a chore? Seems like feeding Mush would be a joy."

"Like feeding Iktae."

"Exactly. And you'd do it happily enough if your parents backed off and trusted you. If they didn't nag. If they didn't fill in for you when you forgot."

Soccer Fan suspected this was true.

"Or if I got to feed him the food he likes to eat. Mush gets the same boring food day after day. My parents say it's not good for a dog to change diets all the time."

Soccer Fan rolled onto his back. The landscape of the ceiling of the cave was familiar to him now, with its bumps and fractures. As he burrowed deeper into his ducky sack, he sighed with contentment. "I'm glad the tides have come back. Now everything will return to normal."

"Until the next time the neaps come," Ideth replied. "Then the Krog Padders will repeat their pitiful performance."

"And I'll have to feed Iktae again."

"Yes," Ideth said. "At the rowboat."

"You know about the rowboat?" he asked.

Ideth laughed. "I certainly do. Who do you think wrecked that boat here, ten years ago, trying to get a findling to the island who flat-out refused to paddle?"

"You?"

Ideth nodded. "Indeed. Remember that boy I told you about, Nathaniel? Well, after I paddled him to the East Ender, he wouldn't go any farther. Wouldn't come to Krog Pad unless I scared up a boat."

"But Nathaniel's the one who almost got eaten by a dodecopus," Soccer Fan pointed out, remembering what Ideth had told him before his first paddle. "I don't blame him!"

Ideth laughed again and said, "Neither do I, truth be told. But he wasn't Nathaniel anymore by then. He'd renamed himself Inhale Ant. And, oh my goodness, that boy had no idea how to use an oar."

17

The Trial of Jimmy Albini

s there DNA evidence linking the suspect, Jimmy Albini, to Frankie's murder?" a grim-faced prosecutor asked his star witness, a petite criminalist named Stella Knight, who sat smugly, clutching a large, intimidating-looking binder.

The courtroom was packed. Frankie's parents sat near the front, holding hands. It had been nearly five months since Frankie had gone missing, and now it was time for justice. They stared angrily at the back of Jimmy Albini's slightly balding head. He was dressed in a loose-fitting orange prison jumpsuit and stared at his feet, looking guilty as sin. He'd been in and out of "the system"—the criminal justice system—since he was a teenager, and he looked the part.

Stella replied pertly, "Yes, there certainly is." She raised a judgmental eyebrow and turned her gaze to Jimmy.

The prosecutor smiled. "I thought so," he said. "Suppose you tell the court about it."

Stella shifted in her chair so she could open the massive binder without losing her balance. The binder had 202 pages, starting with reports from the crime scene investigation team that had collected evidence at the Russo house and ending with her own DNA report, neatly marked with a bright pink paper clip.

"The police collected a mountain of evidence from the crime scene," she said. "But the item in question, the one that implicates Albini, is a dish towel they found in the kitchen, beside the sink. Evidence Item 007. It had a large blood stain on it."

The prosecutor rubbed his chin, as if hearing this information for the first time. "Hmmm... How do you know it's blood?"

"I performed an immunochromatographic test strip assay to prove it, that's how."

The court reporter looked up, dazed.

"Can you spell that for me please?" she asked.

"I-M-M-U-N-O-C-H-R-O-M-A-T-O-G-R-A-P-H-I-C," Stella said crisply, knowing the unfamiliar, complex word would wow the jury.

The court reporter's ridiculously long, curved nails clattered away on the keyboard, somehow hitting their mark cleanly and efficiently—a hammering staccato of bright yellow.

Jimmy slumped in his chair. He was scared of Stella

Knight, with her huge binder and very, very long word.

The court reporter finished her typing with a flourish, signaling she was ready to go on.

"Okay," said the prosecutor, returning to his witness. "Let's pick up where we left off. The red stain on the dish towel was blood. And it was human blood, I presume. Correct?"

"Yes, that's right. Not only was it human, but it was Jimmy Albini's."

"Which means he's the killer?"

The judge shot a warning glance at the prosecutor. His questioning of Stella had gone off the rails. Just because Albini's blood was on the towel didn't mean he'd murdered anyone. That was the jury's call, when all the evidence had been presented to them.

He shifted his gaze to August Slepe, Jimmy's defense attorney, who was snoring lightly in the chair beside his client. Slepe should have objected to the prosecutor's outrageous line of questioning, but he couldn't do so if he was snoozing.

"This is awful for Jimmy," the judge thought sorrowfully. "It's clear the poor young man isn't a child killer. I've seen a few child killers in my day, and Jimmy isn't one of them."

The prosecutor acknowledged the judge's displeasure with a nod, and shifted his strategy. Looking at his notes he asked, "How do you know the blood came from Mr. Albini?"

"I performed autosomal STR typing on the stain and generated an electropherogram," Stella explained, as if everyone in the courtroom, including the bugs on the wall, would, and should, know what she was talking about.

The court reporter paused once more, her nails poised above the keyboard. Two more big words to spell.

The prosecutor looked at the members of the jury. Every one of them appeared to be impressed.

"Okay," the prosecutor continued. "Blood has DNA in it, doesn't it?"

"Yes, it does."

"And DNA testing is very accurate, right?"

"Yes, it is."

"Can you put a weight on the match you made to Albini?" he asked. "How many other people have the same DNA profile as him?"

It was the prosecutor's moment of shining glory, and Stella sat up straight.

"Only one in two hundred octillion," she replied. "There's absolutely no one else in the Universe who could have left that blood on the towel."

"Wow!" cried the prosecutor, as if he'd never discussed this finding with Stella and was shocked at the strength of the evidence. "That's incredible! We need to get Jimmy off the streets, don't we? He mustn't be allowed to murder another helpless kid."

August Slepe's head was flat on his desk. His eyeglasses were askew. His snoring had picked up its tempo, and he appeared to be dreaming.

The judge rose out of his seat and banged his gavel to wake Slepe up.

"C'mon Slepe!" he shouted. "Get with it, man! There were no eyewitnesses to the crime and the police haven't found a body."

Mr. Slepe lifted his head from the desk and gazed around the courtroom with a yawn. Then he reluctantly got to his feet.

"Objection," he said meekly.

"Sustained!" the judge barked in relief. It wasn't the first time he'd presided over a trial where August Slepe was the defense attorney. He knew that Slepe often snoozed when he should have been defending. He was glad the man was able to cough up one objection at least.

Slepe sat down and the prosecutor slyly winked at the jury.

"Never mind," he said. "I think Ms. Knight has made it perfectly clear what happened. On October twenty-first of last year, Albini abducted Frankie. There was a scuffle along the way. Albini hurt his thumb and cleaned it up before he whisked the kid off to who-knows-where."

The judge banged his gavel once more. August Slepe was awake now, but doodling.

"Mr. Slepe? What the heck are you doing? This isn't an art class!"

Slepe looked up, as if surprised to find himself in a courtroom. He didn't say a word as the judge glared at him.

Jimmy winced and looked at his attorney, who'd returned to drawing. He was scribbling a cartoon of Spiderman.

"I'm going to get convicted," Jimmy thought in sudden certainty, the blood draining from his face. "I'll go to prison. I'll be back in the system. Slepe isn't going to save me!"

"Mr. Slepe," the judge continued, this time sarcastically, "it would be lovely if you could join us back here in the courtroom. I think your client would appreciate it."

The prosecutor scoffed, and rolled his eyes at the jury. "I guess Mr. Slepe here believes his client killed Frankie, and doesn't think he's worth defending."

August Slepe had no cross-examination questions for Stella Knight, punctuating the truth in the prosecutor's words.

The trial lasted two weeks, and Frankie's parents attended every day. Witnesses for the prosecution came to the stand, one after another, where the prosecutor cleverly twisted their words without any objection from Mr. Slepe.

An elderly receptionist from Bob's Roofing came to the stand. She liked Jimmy and didn't think he was

capable of abducting and killing a child. She hoped her testimony would help him.

The prosecutor began his questioning.

"Mrs. Wong, on the morning of October twenty-second of last year, did Jimmy Albini arrive at work on time?"

She smiled. "Oh, yes! Jimmy was always on time and a real good worker."

She looked across at Jimmy, gazing at him in a grandmotherly way.

The prosecutor continued. "And on that day, did your boss, Bob Grebes, send him home?"

"Well, yes… yes, he did. But not because Jimmy did anything wrong. It's just that Jimmy's thumb was banged up real bad. Bob thought it wasn't safe for him to work."

"His thumb was banged up *real bad?*" The prosecutor parroted.

"Yes, poor thing."

"Ah. Well, that's most unfortunate, I agree," he continued slyly, egging her on.

"Yes, yes it was. He was repairing a roof, you see. That's where he banged it up. Isn't that a shame?"

Mrs. Wong smiled at Jimmy encouragingly, but the next question stopped her in her tracks.

"Whose roof was he working on? Do you remember?"

"Well, yes… I mean no… I heard about it later, on the news. But Jimmy wouldn't hurt anyone. I'm sure he's not the one you're after."

The prosecutor paused, cracking his knuckles to great effect.

"So, you're asking this jury to believe that Jimmy just *happened* to be working on the Russo's roof the day Frankie disappeared? And that he just *happened* to come to work the next day with a huge, bloody gash on his thumb? You think it's a coincidence? Really?"

Mrs. Wong wasn't too bright. Trapped, she looked around the room in confusion, from the jury to Jimmy, and from Jimmy to the judge, with pleading eyes. "Well... I didn't say it was a huge, bloody gash. I mean, he'd wrapped it up real neat and tidy—"

"Ha!" the prosecutor grunted with satisfaction. "I'm done with this witness. Thanks Mrs. Wong for making it crystal clear who committed the murder."

A few days later, the trial was over and August Slepe hadn't cross-examined any of the prosecution's witnesses or called a single witness of his own.

"Our side's case is so much stronger," Frankie's mother whispered to the prosecutor as final arguments concluded and the jury filed away.

The prosecutor sighed. "It is and it isn't," he explained. "The police don't have a body, and it's very hard to get a murder conviction without one. But that defense attorney was a disaster, so we have a chance."

The jury deliberated for two long days. Frankie's

parents, exhausted from the emotional drama of the trial and the past several months of agony over Frankie's loss, were unable to eat or sleep. It was a terrible time of great uncertainty, but finally they got the expected call.

"The jury's reached a verdict," the prosecutor informed them. "It will be announced this afternoon."

The jury, poker-faced, filed into the courtroom. Frankie's parents gripped each other's hands tightly, praying that they would get some closure, praying that justice would be served for Frankie, who was surely dead. Their dear son. They would have done anything to hug him one last time. Not pester him about his homework. Not accuse him of being lazy. Just hug him and tell him how much they loved him.

The judge asked the jury foreman. "How do you find the defendant?"

The jury foreman cleared his throat.

"As to the count of kidnapping, we find him guilty. We also find him guilty of murder in the first degree."

Having delivered their verdict, every member of the jury swung their eyes in the direction of Jimmy, showering him with judgmental hate.

"Thank God they got him," Roberto whispered as Evelyn broke down and wept in his arms.

It wasn't the outcome the Russos had hoped for. They wanted Frankie to be alive. But they'd given up all hope, and they wanted his murderer to pay for his crime.

For his part, Jimmy was trembling like a leaf. He'd been found guilty. *Guilty.* Betrayed by the system yet again. He tapped August Slepe on the shoulder, to get his attention. He didn't like to bother an important man like a lawyer, but his life was on the line.

"What happens to me now?" he whispered. "Will I go to prison?"

August Slepe snorted. "Are you kidding? Of course you'll go to prison." He stood up and stretched, coming fully awake now that the trial was over.

"But I didn't do it," Jimmy insisted. "I didn't abduct and murder Frankie."

Slepe looked down at Jimmy as he flipped open his briefcase and stuffed his doodles inside. "Child killer!" he spat." Then he shut his briefcase and left the courtroom while a guard put handcuffs on Jimmy.

"Everyone knows you're guilty," the guard grunted. "Even your attorney."

It was true. No one believed in Jimmy but the judge, who looked down on him sorrowfully from his high bench and shook his head. He hated to see an injustice play out in his courtroom. It made him hate his job and wish he was a salesman at Motorcycle Dudes on Main Street or some other line of work where lives weren't on the line.

"Somehow, that man's blood got on a towel in the Russo kitchen," he thought, "and that's a real puzzle. But he's no child killer."

He was right, of course. Jimmy was an innocent man because no crime had actually taken place. As the jury left the courthouse for their own homes, and a police officer hauled Jimmy away to rot in prison, Frankie was quite alive and healthier than ever, enjoying a snack of bluff berry acorn muffins with Iktae, in their secret rowboat, under a bright Krog Pad sky.

18

An Innocent Man

Jimmy Oscar Albini was raised by an angry, abusive stepfather and a mother who couldn't stay sober. Unlike Frankie, he didn't live in a fine house by the sea. Nor was he lucky enough to live in a hut with great-aunts and goats. Instead, he lived in a dangerous part of town in a small apartment over a liquor store. Sometimes there was food in the fridge, but often there wasn't. And the seedy characters who came and went, usually with brown paper bags and rolls of money, scared the living daylights out of him.

His step-father's beatings were daily events, usually in the evenings when Jimmy's mom was hanging out at one of the local bars. Jimmy was the lightning rod for his step-father's aggression, an easy target.

When Jimmy cried out in pain, his stepfather

snapped: "You're useless, kid. You can't do anything right." And because Jimmy had the gift of *Doing Things Right*, his step-father's cruelty devastated him. While another kid with the gift of *Standing Up for the Little Guy* might have learned karate and taken on the abusive man, Jimmy was a gentle soul, and grew up feeling terrible about himself, believing he was a bad egg.

Jimmy joined a gang of local youths when he was eleven. He had no choice if he wanted to survive. The gang provided him protection on the streets and became his pseudo-family, replacing the one he'd never had. Mostly, the gang engaged in petty stuff—vandalism ("playing jokes") and spraying graffiti on buildings and sidewalks ("playing tag"). But there were break ins and burglaries, too, crimes that spelled trouble for Jimmy, even though he didn't plan them and took part reluctantly.

Jimmy was intimidated by the gang leader, a massive twenty-year-old who called himself "King Pin." But he liked him, too, because King Pin saw something in him.

"You've got good hands, kid," King Pin often said, after a successful robbery. "You always get the job done right. Keep it up. The gang's got your back."

As it turned out, the gang didn't have Jimmy's back, not when push came to shove. When Jimmy was fourteen, one of the members ratted him out after a burglary at a convenience store. He never knew for sure who it was, but King Pin never came to visit him in jail, and Jimmy knew he was on his own.

After that, Jimmy bounced in and out of the system for five years. And like most kids in his position, every time he'd bounce in, the prison guards would treat him like he was useless and couldn't do anything right. And every time he bounced out, no one would give him a job because he had a criminal record.

One night, while he was "out" (not in prison), he unwisely accepted a ride from some guys he didn't know very well. Jimmy didn't like the look of the sleazy driver, but he decided to go with the group, anyway. A few minutes later, the driver sped through a red light, skidded across a parking lot, and collided with the brick wall of a police station. It was insanely bad luck to hit such a target, but once done, it couldn't be undone. Jimmy and his "friends" were arrested, and the police searched the car for stolen goods. Sure enough, the cops found the contraband they were looking for, and all the kids were charged with a felony.

The charge didn't stick, at least for Jimmy, but it was an important moment. The police took a cheek cell swab from him while he was in custody. The cops had his DNA and his profile was uploaded into **CODIS**, the national database, where the DNA profiles of hardened criminals from all over the country are stored, along with those of misguided kids like Jimmy, who aren't hardened at all.

After that, Jimmy hated himself more than ever. Despite King Pin's praise, the damage to his self-image had already been done. When a child's parents tell him he's useless and can't do anything right, starting from the time he's very small, it becomes a part of how he sees himself. Jimmy was sure he was flawed, deep inside. He didn't need anyone else to convince him. Not anymore.

When Jimmy was nineteen, though, he got a break. A judge put him in a special program designed to help young repeat offenders learn a trade. The boss of the roofing company, Bob Grebes, wasn't thrilled with taking him on, but the government compensation for hiring Jimmy was enough to convince him.

Bob was hard on Jimmy at first, but over time, he noticed that Jimmy never left a nail sticking out or a leak unsealed. Bob's Roofing, he decided, needed more employees like Jimmy, even if they had a criminal record. So, he offered Jimmy a full-time job, welcoming him to the company with a handshake and an advance of one hundred dollars. Jimmy didn't think he was worthy of rescue, but he grabbed the lifeline.

Bob was good to Jimmy, but he kept his distance. He'd never been in the system himself and was wary of people who had. When company holiday parties came around, he asked Jimmy not to attend. It was hard on Jimmy, but he understood. Why would someone want to hang out with a worthless person like himself?

Jimmy rarely went out, except to go to work, and he kept to himself even there. In the evenings, he ate his microwaved dinners in front of the TV with his sole companion: an overweight, multi-toed cat he called King Pin. He was a sad, lonely person who didn't feel worthy of the ratty little couch he sat on. But he was safe from the system. Blessedly safe.

The only bright light in his day was when he encountered Sara, an employee at a local deli. She had four sisters and a big extended family, which appealed to Jimmy very much. She became his first real friend, and he developed a crush on her.

"When's your birthday, Jimmy?" she asked him one day, when he came in for a sandwich.

"January eleventh," he told her. "But I never celebrate it."

"That's sad," she said, gazing at him with warm brown eyes. "January eleventh is coming right up, and everyone deserves a birthday party. I'll organize it."

Jimmy's heart skipped a beat, and suddenly he felt courageous and took a big risk.

"Would you like to go out sometime?" he asked. He'd been wanting to ask her on a date for seven months, and the words just popped out.

She smiled and cocked her head to one side.

"You're a nice man, Jimmy," she said. "But I don't like you like that."

Jimmy slunk home and shut himself in his bathroom,

looking into the mirror. "You're useless!" he shouted to his image. "You can't do anything right!"

It was only a week later that the police arrested him for Frankie's abduction and murder, while he was carefully affixing tiles to the roof of a newly constructed tire store. He knew he hadn't done anything wrong, and he felt terrible for Frankie's parents. But because he felt so bad about himself, he didn't bother to look up the professional record of the public defender assigned to his case. He simply put his fate in August Slepe's incapable hands and figured he probably deserved whatever he got.

August Slepe had graduated last in his class from a third-rate online law school and was well known for being a lousy attorney. He was lazy, jaded, and sure all his clients were guilty. Thus, he never interviewed Jimmy to figure out how his blood might have gotten on the towel in the Russo's kitchen in an innocent way. Instead, he assumed Jimmy was a scumbag and not worthy of a capable defense.

Another attorney, who'd graduated at the top of her class at a first-rate law school and taken careful notes in court, wouldn't have been so hasty. She'd have gotten to know Jimmy and would have realized he wasn't capable of hurting a kid. She would have asked him about the day he was working on the Russo's roof, and about the bloody towel. She would have realized that Jimmy hadn't graduated from high school and had no idea that blood contained DNA. Then together, as a team, they would have built a defense. The initial exchange between them might have gone like this:

Attorney: Tell me about how you hurt your thumb."

Jimmy: "When I was working on the Russo's roof, I accidentally drove a nail through it. I guess I hit a vessel or something because when I pulled the nail out, it bled like crazy. So, I climbed down my ladder and knocked on the front door. A kid opened it—I think it was Frankie—and he stopped the bleeding with a towel. Maybe when he took the towel back inside, he left it in the kitchen. Does that explain the DNA?"

Attorney: "Yes, Jimmy. I believe it does."

BINGO!

The truth was as simple as that. On the day that Frankie went missing, he didn't go directly back to his room after washing the "Lush Lavender" stain off his finger. Instead, he answered a knock at the front door. Helping Jimmy staunch the bleeding was easy, and when he was done, he discarded the towel on the kitchen counter, thinking nothing of it.

Thus, Officer Morgan thought he'd arrested the right man, and Jimmy was convicted for a crime that never happened.

The judge would have thrown out the case had he known, but, as it was, Jimmy had no hope. So, he resigned himself to being back in the system for life

without parole, spending his days confined to a sagging cot, trying to block out the obnoxious snoring of his cellmate, Big Bud, and writing love letters to Sara in his mind.

Jimmy had no hope…

19

The Storm

Uh, oh. We're in for a big one," warned Ideth one morning, peering out of the cave, squinting at the sky. "Nasty storm."

The monsoon season had swept in and they'd had squalls every day for several weeks. But the black, angry clouds hunched on the horizon this time were different. The storm was massive and coming directly at them. It would hit landfall in a matter of hours.

"I love storms!" Soccer Fan cried happily.

"I usually do, too," Ideth agreed. "But this one's coming at a bad time. We're in a trilogy right now. A syzygy when both moons are new. The storm surge could be massive."

Soccer Fan didn't share Ideth's appreciation for the risk. "Trilogies are great," he said. "Stars-gazing all night with the Krog Padders is fun. I know the names of the constellations now: *We See Three*, *Big Beast Be*, and *Like Seahorse Is*. The bright star high in the west at sunset is called *Up Be?*"

Ideth roared with laughter.

"*Up Be?*" she repeated, doubling over with glee. "Oh, oh... ha ha... that's hilarious!"

Soccer Fan couldn't help but laugh along, though he had no idea what had struck Ideth as funny. Her laughter was infectious.

"It's not a star," Ideth explained when she caught her breath. "It's a planet that lies between Urth and the sun. Like your planet Venus, it shifts between the morning and evening skies. On Cairntip, we have charts that predict its behavior. We don't wonder when it's going to be visible or not. But the Krog Padders, with no astronomy and no way to envision the future, have no idea what's going to happen. *Up Be?* Oh, I think my sides are going to split open! It's so Krog Padderish!"

Soccer Fan got the joke now, and joined in her mirth. He didn't know much about Venus, but he got her point.

When they'd recovered from their laughter, Ideth explained that *Up Be?* was a planet called Celestia, and had three moons.

Soccer Fan thought, "Three moons? What would they call the moons-light there? *Moons-lights*, maybe? He imagined himself as the Chief Astronomer on Celestia, draped in a magnificent satin robe, poised at the eyepiece of a mighty telescope.

"The moons are Franeik, Iekfran, and Knarfie," he imagined telling a young apprentice. "One is red, one is blue, and one is purple."

Ideth laughed.

"Name one of them Ideth," she requested. "I only ask that one of the moons be renamed for me."

Soccer Fan said, "Okay, Knarfie is now Ideth. I'll make a note in my astronomer's log." Then, leaving fantasy behind in favor of the beach and the coming storm, Soccer Fan left the cave.

"Be back before noon," Ideth warned him as he rounded the corner and started down. "You won't want to be caught outside when the storm gets here, believe me."

Soccer Fan climbed his switchback trail ("the slow one" Ideth called it) in an expansive state of mind. He wanted to feel the wind whip back his hair and revel in the smell of the coming rain. His parents owned a vacation cottage in Mendocino, about three hundred miles north of Monterey. Storms were common there, and he liked to sneak up to the third floor, under the eaves, to watch the rain pelt sidewise onto the window glass. Sometimes he opened the window and hung his feet out, pretending he was on a ship rounding the Cape of Good Hope. Or he might spin around the big globe by the fire and daydream about mysterious places: Easter Island, The Marshall Islands, The Cayman Islands, Jamaica, Kenya, Norfolk Island, and impossibly distant and exotic Tasmania.

A storm on Krog Pad Island, at a trilogy, promised to be even more exciting. It would be a real whopper. He couldn't wait.

When he got to the end of his trail, he looked around for his duppies, but the beach was strangely empty. The tide was coming in, *way* in. Soon, the beach would be a narrow strip of rocky land hugging the contour of the mountain. But they were nowhere to be seen. He walked down the beach to the boat wreck to look for Iktae, but she wasn't there. It wasn't time for the Krog Padders to flop, but he checked their usual flop spot, anyway. Nothing.

"Weird," he thought. "Where've they gone?"

Soccer Fan wandered up the beach for about a quarter mile in one direction, turned around, and then headed back.

He'd been walking with the wind behind him, he realized, because when he turned around, the strength of it caught him by surprise. Sand flew directly at him and he had to squint and turn his head to the side to avoid getting it in his eyes.

That's when he spotted them: The Krog Padders, standing side-by-side, in a long line, holding hands, facing the bluff.

Soccer Fan was stunned. He'd never seen his duppies behave like this before. He had no idea what it meant. Was it some kind of ritual? Goodness knows they had some bizarre beliefs. They thought that gulls brought the sun up in the morning (*Gull fly! Sun sky!*) and that moons-eclipses spelled disaster. They were horrified when Lunera passed in front of Ru, screaming "*No Ru! Die you!*" as they buried their heads in the sand. Yet nothing bad ever happened. As soon as the eclipse had passed, they forgot all about the supposed "danger."

Both superstitions were clearly wrong. Soccer Fan didn't know enough about gravity and Newton's Laws to refute the first, but he tried to convince them of the folly of the second. He reminded the Krog Padders that nothing bad had happened after the last moons-eclipse, but they'd given him blank stares.

"SHUM! SHUM!" Soccer Fan shouted, over the sound of the wind. "LOOK AT ME! LOOK AT ME! WHY YOU NO HAPPY BE?"

Shum turned to him, his usually exuberantly happy face a mask of terror.

"NO SEE! NOT BE!" he wailed, as if he were in pain. Then he turned back toward the bluff and squeezed his eyes shut again, rigid as a stone.

"NO SEE! NOT BE!" wailed a woman farther on down the line. Her eyes were squeezed shut, too, as were the eyes of all the Krog Padders.

The chorus quickly swelled, as Krog Padders up and down the line repeated the phrase, in low male voices, higher women's voices, and the squeaky voices of their children: "NO SEE! NOT BE!"

A large cloud fell across the face of the sun, casting the beach into shadow. The temperature dropped a full ten degrees in a matter of moments.

Iktae was facing the bluff, too, standing in front of Shum, behaving the same way. He squatted down to her eye level and shook her, but she ignored him. Over and over again she whimpered "NO SEE! NOT BE!" oblivious, it seemed, to her surroundings.

Soccer Fan was utterly confused and decided to ask Ideth what was going on. She'd likely offer up some silly explanation and they'd both laugh. Still, goose bumps popped up on the back of his neck.

Soccer Fan left his duppies and climbed back to the cave. He stopped halfway up and looked out to sea, surprised at how quickly the storm was progressing.

"It will hit land soon," he thought excitedly. "I'd better get a move on."

When he reached the cave and looked inside, Ideth wasn't there. She was out gathering Krog Pad acorns, he assumed. They were ripe now, and she'd promised to take one last trip topside, to get some, before the storm arrived. Soccer Fan thought she was cutting the time perilously close, and went to find her.

He spotted her a short way up the bluff, coming down, her backpack stuffed with acorns. Her hair was whipping this way and that as gusts of sudden wind struck her from odd angles. She was trying to keep her wild mane under control with her free hand.

Soccer Fan rushed up to meet her, taking her backpack so she could focus on her descent. When they reached a safe spot, he put the pack down and turned to her.

"MY DUPPIES ARE ACTING STRANGE!" he yelled above the wind. "THEY'RE STANDING IN A LINE, HOLDING HANDS, FACING THE BLUFF, AND SHOUTING 'NO SEE! NOT BE!' WHAT DOES IT MEAN?"

Ideth was nonplussed. She seemed to know all about it.

She shouted back, "STORM AT TRILOGY!"

She pointed to the cave and raised her eyebrows, signaling that they should go there to talk. Soccer Fan nodded and led the way down. By the time they made it back to the cave, where it was relatively windless and quiet, the sky was dark and menacing.

A raindrop splashed on Soccer Fan's arm. He felt another hit his bare shoulder. The sky flashed white as a bolt of lightning split the canopy of angry clouds rolling in overhead. A few seconds later, thunder boomed all around.

Soccer Fan and Ideth hurried into the cave, barely escaping the deluge that followed. The storm was upon them, and Ideth quickly flipped on her hurricane lamp so they could see what they were doing.

Soccer Fan made his way to the cooking pit. He was getting cold and had no warm clothing.

"Can I make a fire?" he asked uncertainly, eyeing the fissure high above. Rain water was already leaking through, trickling down the curved cave wall. A slender stream.

Ideth replied, "You can. This cave is shaped so the water will cascade off to one side and empty into a chasm below. We can cook and stay warm during a storm in a happy cave like this."

Soccer Fan imagined himself a bug, carried along by the water, down through the deep recesses below the cave and out through a crack in the bluff. He'd surf his way out, he decided, on a blue body board, competing with fellow bugs to see who could reach the ocean first. He grinned at the very idea.

Amused, Ideth joined him at the fire pit, adding a couple of logs and a twist on his fantasy.

"I'll surf my way out on an *orange* board, thank you very much," she said, "buck naked all the way. Am I right, or am I right?"

The fire flamed to life and Soccer Fan blew on it to fuel it with oxygen. He'd found that encouraging a fire early on paid dividends later. During his time on Urth, he'd become quite skilled at starting and tending a fire, and if he'd had great aunts and goats to care for, he'd have managed just fine.

He took up residence beside the fire, warming his hands. He'd momentarily forgotten about the disturbing behavior of his duppies, caught up in the drama and excitement of the storm.

He was reminded when Ideth plopped down beside him and said, "'NO SEE, NOT BE,' eh? Well, I'm not surprised."

Soccer Fan eyed her curiously.

"What does it mean?"

"Well, it's a sad tale and one I hoped I'd never have to tell. But now that there's a storm at trilogy, you need to know the truth."

Soccer Fan leaned in.

"Go on," he said. Ideth, he sensed, was about the reveal the secret she'd been holding from him. The reason why Krog Padder children renamed themselves early.

Ideth sighed, inching herself a bit closer. "You know how the Krog Padders make no preparations for the neap tides? They frolic and play while the seafood is in front of them and starve when it goes away? It's very short-sighted, and I say that's okay as long as they're willing to pay the price. They go hungry for a few days, and it's pretty pitiful, but soon enough they're back to normal."

Soccer Fan nodded. "They go right back to 'Happy be!'"

"Yes, they do. And all is well. But…"

"But what?"

She took a deep breath and exhaled slowly before she continued.

"Well, they don't prepare for storms like this, either. They don't build and maintain trails up to safe caves like this one. Instead, they're stuck out on the beach, and it's not just a matter of going hungry for a few days.

People have tried to help them. But the Krog Padders just won't listen."

Soccer Fan sprang to his duppies' defense.

"They *can't* listen, Ideth. It's not their fault. I wish you'd stop blaming them for being who they are. Their brains can't see into the future."

Ideth didn't respond, and Soccer Fan sat back down and grew quiet. Ideth was so judgmental about the Krog Padders. She was always talking about "gifts" and findlings and what-not. Why didn't she see that the Krog Padders had a gift of their own? What was it? The gift of *Happy Be,* perhaps? The gift of *Living for Today*? The gift of *Here and Now*?

"Maybe," he thought, "the gift of *Fantasy*. Just like me."

The rain drummed on the ground outside the cave. The surf was weirdly loud. The furor of the storm was surprising. But Soccer Fan was inside, safe and dry. After his earlier chill, he was warming up. His feet were toasty. The acorns smelled sweet, their aroma mixed with the urthy smell of rain.

Just like me.

"You know what, Ideth?" he said, struck by a sudden idea. "Back in Monterey, I'm a Krog Padder."

Ideth nodded. "Children with the gift of *Fantasy* usually are."

"We're all Krog Padders. Me and my duppies. Mush, too."

"That's right. The lot of you."

Ideth picked up a stick and stirred the fire. "The thing is, your duppies have no one to save them when they get lost in their fun fantasies. They don't have owners or parents to step in and take care of practical things. During the neaps they starve, and during storms, well..."

"Well what?" Soccer Fan asked, unconcerned. "I guess they paddle, right? What do they care about a storm surge? They'll ride the swells, having a blast. I wish I could be with them."

In his mind's eye, Shum was cresting a huge wave with Iktae on his shoulders. Iktae was grinning ear to ear, about to dive under. He was jealous. He wished he could hold his breath for up to thirty minutes. He imagined himself learning how to do it, and surprising Andreas and Paulo at the next water polo tournament, paddling right past them at light speed, never having to come up for air.

"No, honey," Ideth said softly, correcting him. "It's not like that."

Soccer Fan looked into Ideth's eyes to get his bearings. *Honey.* She'd never called him that before. And her voice sounded sad, so terribly sad. That was new to him, too.

A prickle of fear crawled up his spine when he realized that she was crying. He'd never seen her cry. Not even close.

Soccer Fan fought down a growing panic.

"What do you mean?" he asked evenly. "What happens to my duppies in storms like this?"

Then, when Ideth didn't answer immediately, he

repeated, more loudly and urgently: "What happens to them, Ideth?"

Ideth didn't lower her eyes. She held his gaze.

"Have you ever wondered why there are so few children on this island?" she asked.

He nodded. "Sure, I've wondered a time or two. Out of sixty-two adults, there are only six kids. I guess it's a bit odd, but the Krog Padders seem content. They never talk about children unless a child is right in front of them."

Ideth continued, her eyes growing wet with tears, "For good reason, Soccer Fan. Most of their children die. They drown."

Soccer Fan frowned. "I don't understand. What do you mean? Urth people can't drown. How could they? You yourself told me that you'd do fine in storms like this."

"Adults rarely drown, that's true, but children are different. Their bodies are immature. They need their parents to keep them safe when paddling. That's why we have tufts for them to cling onto. If they get separated from their parents… Well it's not good. The Krog Padders lose their children in storms like this. The storm surge rips them from their parents and they're carried out to sea."

"They don't plan," Soccer Fan said, suddenly understanding. "They don't notice the danger until it's almost upon them!"

Ideth nodded. "And there's no one to step in and rescue them. When the storms at syzygies come, the best they can do is to squeeze their eyes shut and try to pretend *it's not going to happen.* That's why they cry 'NO SEE! NOT BE!' It's their way of coping. But that's all over now. The tides are nearly in."

Soccer Fan whipped his head around, leapt to his feet, and raced to look out of the cave. Far below, under a pitch-black sky roiling with clouds and blinding rain, the sound of the storm surge was deafening. A bolt of lightning suddenly lit the sky, and for one illuminated moment, Soccer Fan saw it all: Boiling, ugly water racing toward what was left of the beach, directly toward the bluffs, with astonishing power and speed.

"IKTAE!" he screamed.

20

Saving Iktae

Horrified, Soccer Fan grabbed Ideth's hurricane lamp, shot through the mouth of the cave, and disappeared. He had no plan. He operated purely on instinct. His goal was to get to Iktae as fast as he could, no matter the cost.

His usual trail down to the beach, a hike of a few miles, crossed the exposed topside of the bluff before switchbacking down a ridge. If he took it, he'd be at the complete mercy of the storm and it might take him hours to get to the beach. Even Ideth's shorter, more precipitous route would be too slow. Instead, he headed in the opposite direction, directly into the ferocious wind and blinding rain, along a ledge about twenty feet wide, towards the only viable alternative.

The ledge offered no protection from the storm's howling fury. With gusts of more than fifty miles per hour, the wind dislodged tumbleweeds and bluff debris, sending them flying directly into Soccer Fan's path. He leaned his shoulder into the wind and turned his head to one side to shield his eyes. It was the only way to make any progress and protect himself from serious injury.

Twice, he stopped and hunched down, sure that if he remained upright, he'd be blown off the ledge altogether. His loin cloth whipped against his thighs.

In the black trilogy night, devoid of moons, his only reliable source of light was Ideth's hurricane lamp. Between gusts, he held it up so he could stay on course. It was an electric light, thank goodness, not an oil lamp with a flame that would have been extinguished in a heartbeat. Still, he was terrified that it would blink out at any moment, plunging him into utter darkness. His only hope, then, would be the flashes of lightning that ripped through the angry clouds at unpredictable intervals and offered brief glimpses of the chaos, followed almost instantly by deep rumbles of thunder that were far too close.

He paused for only a moment at the top of the narrow chute, as the enormity of what he was about to do sunk in. It was the same airy-scary fissure that had terrified him months before, when he'd been marooned on the bluff by Ideth. Normally, he'd never have attempted to descend it, much less in a trilogy storm, but now there was no other option. It offered a direct route to the spot where he'd last seen the Krog Padders, and all that mattered was saving Iktae in time. It might be too late already. He hadn't a moment to lose.

Acrophobia is a debilitating condition. Soccer Fan had seen parents at the Just Hangin' Out Rock Gym slip their susceptible children little orange pills to calm their nerves before competitions. He wished he had a whole bottle full of those pills now. But he was alone at the narrow entrance to the vertiginous chute. The helpful, hovering parents at the Just Hangin' Out Rock Gym were 64,000 light years away. They had no idea what he was doing. They didn't even know where he was.

He sized up the situation immediately and knew that he'd have to navigate the dizzying route backwards. Otherwise, he was sure to pitch forward into the empty abyss and tumble off into nothingness. And he also realized that he'd be leaving Ideth's hurricane lamp behind, his only source of comfort. He'd need all four limbs to climb. Her lamp would only make his descent more supremely perilous than it already was.

So, with his heart banging and his head spinning, he flicked off the lamp, secured it under a nearby boulder so it wouldn't blow away, and prepared to make his next move. He was furious at Ideth for putting him in such a death-defying situation. If she'd warned him about syzygy storms weeks ago, when they'd first arrived on Krog Pad (which she could have done!), he'd have prepared, in advance, to protect the Krog Pad children. Instead, she was so snooty about the Krog Padders that she let it slide. Now, Iktae's survival was all up to him.

Taking a deep breath as his bowels loosened with terror, he turned around and grabbed two secure rocks with his hands so he could ease himself over the edge. Then blindly, for he couldn't see his feet, he searched for footholds below. His left foot reached a promising out-cropping, but the moment he put weight on it, it crumbled out from under him. He had better luck with his right foot. The rock beneath it held firm. Both his legs were shaking and he felt sick to his stomach. What was he thinking? Was he crazy? He almost scrambled back up to safety, but thinking of Iktae, he bravely fought down his terror. He had to go on.

Always maintain three points of contact. That's what the instructors at the Just Hangin' Out Rock Gym told the kids. Soccer Fan had heard them often enough at Alex's climbing competitions. Their advice came rushing back to him now. His two hands and his right foot were his "three points" as he blindly groped again to find purchase with his left foot. When he finally found a foothold that didn't shift, he took a moment to breathe deeply. *Four points of contact now.*

He tried to relax, but suddenly he remembered another word of caution from Alex's gym instructors.

Don't be stupid. Never free solo a route.

"Free soloing," he knew, was climbing without protection, with no rope to arrest a climber should they fall.

Screw it. He had no choice.

Soccer Fan was not wearing a pair of the upscale, sticky-soled "Granite Planet" climbing shoes that Alex and the other kids on the Just Hangin' Out Sport Climbing Team wore when they scaled the gym walls. Nor did he have a colorful bag of chalk on his hip to absorb the moisture on his hands to improve his grip. In fact, any comparison to Alex's super-safe climbs at the Just Hangin' Out Rock Gym would have been ludicrous. The gym took pride in safety. "Safety First" was their motto, and all the parents had to sign liability forms three pages long before their kids could get near the walls. No one signed a liability form for Soccer Fan as he made his awful descent into the chute with no one to belay him. No parent would have been so negligent. So insane.

Inching his way down, he felt an overwhelming sense of impending doom. The farther he descended into the ominous cleft, the more precarious his situation became. His heart banged like a bass drum. His hands shook. His legs scissored with fear. But once he'd made the commitment to his chosen path, there was no going back. It didn't even cross his mind to abort his journey once he was more than a dozen feet into the chasm.

Soccer Fan had a few things going for him. First, the chute, being surrounded on three sides, was largely protected from the wind and driving rain. Second, when he got stuck, unsure where to put his hands next, a blinding flash of lightning would illuminate the rockface, revealing possibilities that might have eluded him otherwise. He also had some experience climbing now, thanks to Ideth. He wasn't an expert by any stretch of the imagination, but he wasn't a newbie, either.

A blinding flash of lightning would
illuminate the rockface...

Down he went, trying to keep the "three points of contact" rule in his mind. But after a few minutes, he realized that this safe, carefully orchestrated method was far too slow. So, from one crumbly handhold and potentially fatal foothold to the next, above a dizzying funnel of open air, he picked up speed. It didn't matter so much, then, if a handhold or foothold was weak and gave way. Almost as soon as he'd made contact, he was already on to the next.

Every now and then he reached a safe spot, where he could momentarily rest, catch his breath, and work to calm himself. He tried not look down at such times. He couldn't see much anyway. The chute curved in such a way that the beach wasn't in his direct line of sight. But he could hear the roar of the surf intensify as he descended, so he knew he was making progress.

About halfway down, he suddenly lost all four handholds and footholds at the same time and his frantic attempts to find new ones were unsuccessful. He started to slide, but by sheer luck, his loincloth caught on an outcropping and arrested his descent. It was made of an ultra-strong stretchy material. It didn't rip, and for a few surreal seconds, he hung from the garment like a spider from a web, bouncing up and down above the yawning chasm, before he awkwardly regained his holds on the rockface.

Breathe.

Soccer Fan was so focused on his task that he lost

track of time. His entire attention was riveted on staying alive so he could reach Iktae before she was lost to the sea. It might have been eons from his perspective, but, in truth, it didn't take him long to make the audacious journey. He descended fifteen hundred feet in ten minutes. Perhaps it was only eight.

About a hundred feet above the beach, perched in a semi-safe spot for a second, a flash of lightning illuminated the remainder of his path. He could see the beach clearly now. The chute was less steep and flattened out as it emptied into the churning surf below. In an instant, he decided to save time by sliding on his butt the rest of the way, abandoning all caution. It was the craziest, bravest thing he'd ever done, and when he finally careened into the waist-deep, swirling, foamy water, which now covered the entire beach, he couldn't quite believe he was still in one piece.

To his relief, the Krog Padders were still there, standing side-by-side facing the bluff, just as he'd left them. He was only a few yards south of them, and, as soon as he'd regained his footing, he immediately sloshed his way north, through the maelstrom, directly toward them.

The Krog Padders' didn't see him arrive. Their eyes were still screwed shut. Piteously, they cried "NO SEE! NOT BE!" even as the angry ocean swirled around their bodies, threatening to carry them away.

A wave rushed in, and Soccer Fan suddenly found himself underwater as the storm surge slammed him into the bluff. He wasn't seriously injured, but the powerful undercurrent that followed could have easily sucked him out to sea. Fortunately, the long line of rigid Krog Padders offered some protection. The undertow carried him straight into one of the larger Krog Padder men, who was still upright and secure in his position. As the wave retreated and the storm surge threatened to serve up another, Soccer Fan regained his footing and headed straight for Iktae, who wasn't far off, still standing in front of Shum, but now flat up against his body. Shum didn't seem to know she was there.

As soon as Soccer Fan reached them, he grabbed Iktae and, in the same swift motion, switched directions and sloshed his way back toward the chute. If he could reach it before the next wave hit, they might have a chance.

Out of the corner of his eye, Soccer Fan saw the monstrous wave coming. It was a rogue one, higher and more powerful than the rest. He was terrified, and picked up speed. The adrenalin pumping through his body gave him the final boost that he needed, and just as the wave smashed into the bluff with a deafening "BOOM!" he reached the chute and shot inside. A quick climb of ten feet took him and Iktae to safety as the foamy water churned and roiled beneath them. In horror, he watched helplessly as the body of a young child raced by and immediately disappeared. Most of the adult Krog Padders were swept off their feet, too, and, when another flash of lightning zig-zagged through the mammoth night, Soccer Fan could see that it was all over. Not one Krog Padder remained standing. The rogue wave had upended them all.

"DADDY! DADDY!" Iktae wailed, trying to wriggle out of Soccer Fan's grasp. She'd come out of her "NO SEE, NOT BE" stupor and seemed to know exactly what was happening.

But he held her tight, and after a few seconds, she stopped her futile resistance.

"I'VE GOT YOU, IKTAE!" he yelled, as she burrowed her head into his chest. "YOU'RE SAFE NOW. HANG ON!"

In truth, their situation was anything but safe, and it suddenly dawned on Soccer Fan that the task before him was impossible. How could he climb the chute with Iktae? He'd have to ferry her up to one of the resting spots he'd found during his descent. Perhaps they could hunker down there and wait out the worst. He suspected that the storm surge would rise higher. Much higher, in fact, and he was right. They needed to gain altitude quickly to survive.

But even as he plotted a course for such a spot, he realized there was another danger, this one from above. Heavy rains had loosened rocks high in the fissure, and now they started tumbling down. Two of them, as big as baseballs, careened off the walls and missed them by only a couple of feet.

They couldn't retreat back to the beach. The conditions down there were even more hazardous. The only way out of their terrible predicament was up. "Lock your arms around my neck and your legs around my waist," Soccer Fan instructed her loudly. "Hold on tight. You'll be okay." He doubted his words of comfort were true. The chances they'd survive were slim at best. But Iktae did as she was told, and soon Soccer Fan was scrambling upward, hoping against hope that his luck would hold. Iktae's head was pressed against his chest, her arms were wrapped around his neck, and her legs were wrapped around his waist. This left his hands and feet free to climb. He couldn't have made any progress otherwise.

Few mountaineers, on Urth or Earth, had ever faced a more perilous ascent. Not only did Soccer Fan have to get himself to the top of the vertical chute in the terrible storm conditions, but he had to carry Iktae to safety, too. Rain cascaded down the right side of the fissure and made it impossible for him to secure handholds and footholds there, and rockfall was a constant, deadly threat from above. When Soccer Fan heard the sickening sound of stones and boulders tumbling their way, he flattened himself against the rockface, taking care not to crush tiny Iktae. In each terrifying instance, the missiles cascaded past them, sometimes clearing Soccer Fan's head by only a few inches. One stone, the size of a golf ball, landed squarely on his shoulder with a sickening "crack!" before ricocheting off the rock walls like a pinball as it continued on down. But he labored on in spite of the hairline fracture in his clavicle, and his terror that the next shower of rocks that careened down the chute would knock them into the void, back to the horrors of the storm surge below.

Once again, time became weirdly distorted. Each handhold and foothold upward seemed to take forever. He set short-term goals, choosing a landmark not far ahead, telling himself, "If I can just get there, I can stop and rest." But every time he achieved his aim, he wasn't sure why he'd set the goal in the first place. He couldn't rest. It was unthinkable. So, instead, he would just set another goal and continue on up.

Several times he thought he saw the lip of the fissure come into view, and each time it was a false alarm. At one such disappointment, he almost quit, but he told himself, "I've come this far. I can't fail Iktae now."

He started to hallucinate. Driven by sustained exposure to near-death conditions, his mind played tricks on him. A Nice Gal suddenly materialized beside him with a smile and a warm bowl of soup, then vanished into thin air. From high above, Laup shouted "Catch this!" and threw him a lifeline that instantly disappeared.

It's amazing what the human body, especially a young one, can endure when pushed to the limits. The skin on Soccer Fan's fingers and toes was raw and bleeding. His muscles burned with exhaustion and every time he moved his shoulder he felt a sharp jolt of pain. How

long he could have continued on is anyone's guess, but surely, at some point his body would have failed him. The relief he felt when he finally reached the top of the chute and crawled out onto the flat ledge was beyond imagining. At first, he thought he must be dreaming.

The wind and rain smacked into him as soon as he emerged from the chute, but Soccer Fan barely noticed. Now that the climb was over, his body erupted in pain. Everything hurt all at once.

With Iktae still wrapped 'round him, he crawled across the flat ledge, putting as much distance between them and the yawning mouth of the chute as he could. Then he sat down, his back secure against the towering bluff as the enormity of what he'd just accomplished sunk in. They'd reached the top. *They'd done it!* He hugged Iktae and held her close. She was going to be all right, thanks to him.

For three glorious minutes (or was it ten?), Soccer Fan hugged Iktae while he caught his breath and let his adrenalin subside, telling her again and again, as he smoothed her hair, how brave she'd been. How well she'd done. How much he loved her. But he didn't dare delay too long. Iktae was shivering and needed first aid immediately. Their ordeal wouldn't fully be over until they were safe inside the cave. So, with every last ounce of strength he had left, he got back to his feet, retrieved Ideth's hurricane lamp, and flipped it on. Then he carried Iktae along the ledge, his legs wobbling with exhaustion, his feet aflame with pain, holding the lantern up to light his way, not far from their destination now.

With the wind at his back, his progress was speedy, and soon he spied a faint, flickering glow ahead. The mouth of the cave was radiant from the roaring campfire within, and he made a bee-line for it.

When he reached it, he cried out for Ideth, and she appeared almost instantly. It was obvious that she'd been worried sick. Her eyes were red from crying. It took her a moment to realize that he had Iktae, but when she did, her eyes flew open wide with astonishment.

"You *saved* her!" she cried, rushing over to help him. "Oh, I can't believe it! How is it possible?"

She didn't wait for a reply. She could see that Iktae's condition was critical, and she unburdened Soccer Fan immediately and set to work on her, wrapping her up in a ducky sack, placing her in front of the fire, and blowing on her tiny hands to warm them up. Then she towel-dried Iktae's soggy black hair and clipped it into a pony tail, out of the way.

Soccer Fan watched, and when he could see that Iktae was coming around and responding well to Ideth's care, he finally dropped his guard. Liberated of his huge responsibility and too exhausted to speak, he collapsed to the floor of the cave and dissolved in tears.

21

Soccer Fan Makes a Decision

T he storm raged all night and was a terrible one—the worst in decades. They could see the horrific damage when they looked down on the beach at dawn.

Ideth asked Soccer Fan, "Can you manage the trip down the bluff?"

"Yes, of course," he said. "I'm beat up, I admit that, and my shoulder hurts like heck. But I can make it. We need to help the Krog Padders."

Ideth assured Iktae that she'd make it down to the beach safely, too.

"I was mighty worried about you last night, little one, but you're recovered now. Your parents will be frantic, searching for you. Stay with me on the descent, and you'll be back in their arms very soon."

Iktae nodded, though she didn't quite understand. She remembered her parents, and missed them, but she couldn't quite imagine a reunion.

Ideth had spent the night alternately attending to the Iktae's hypothermia and Soccer Fan's injuries, and organizing her backpack. She didn't know what they'd need on the beach, so she packed up everything. Her first aid kit would come in handy, as would her sewing supplies.

"Not meant for stitching up blubber and webbing," she thought. "But the needle and thread will do in a pinch."

As Ideth, Soccer Fan, and Iktae descended the bluff, they could see washed-up debris everywhere. Whole trees had been slammed into the island by the storm surge, splintering like matches. Their two trails had been obliterated; they had to forge a new one. Switchback after switchback, they wound their way down, taking their time. Their progress was slow and exhausting, but when they reached the beach, they were in reasonably good shape, ready to help the Krog Padders in any way that they could.

Slowly, over the course of the morning, Soccer Fan's duppies began appearing, in ones and twos, bedraggled, some bleeding, none of them "Happy be!" Soccer Fan didn't see any children, though the distraught parents were looking for them desperately, under tree branches, in piles of sand, and up against the bluffs, where they might have been carried and smashed by the waves.

Ideth tended to the more serious injuries, while Soccer Fan helped the Krog Padders in their searching. Shum and Dyla were beside themselves with joy when they saw Iktae, and they thanked Soccer Fan again and again when they learned he was responsible for saving her.

Others weren't so lucky.

"Bella go," Dubdy said flatly, grieving the loss of his toddler daughter. "Sea take her." Then, he wept on Soccer Fan's shoulder, drowning in shame and sorrow.

Four children had been found by mid-afternoon: two dead, one near-death but hanging on with Ideth's help, and one (Iktae) miraculously alive.

Ideth said kindly to the parents, "Like as not, they never knew what hit them. The storm surge came quickly—you saw that. They didn't suffer."

Soccer Fan stopped looking for missing children and turned his attention to the living. What else could he do? Ideth had finally stepped off her judgmental perch. She pitched in. Together, they gathered food and built a bonfire. They cooked the Krog Padders dinner.

The surviving Krog Padders gathered around their campfire, sniffing the air. But it wasn't a "Happy be!" kind of sniffing. It was a downcast, shame-filled sniffing.

"They're grieving, but they'll snarf up the food quickly enough," Ideth predicted. "First cooked meal they've had in ages, if ever."

She was right. The Krog Padders lost no time.

Soccer Fan wanted to scream, "YOU DID THIS TO

YOUR OWN CHILDREN!" But he knew it would be cruel. At sunset, Ideth remarked, "They won't learn from it." Soccer Fan had already heard a couple of his duppies shout "Happy be!" (if somewhat dejectedly) and had to agree.

"It makes me sick," he grumbled, poking at the fire with a branch from one of the washed-up trees. "I see how completely disgusting all this is, but I still like them. Somehow, I still like them."

"Me, too," Ideth said.

The fire burned down, and the Krog Padders disappeared to their flop site. Iktae went with them; her parents didn't want her out of their sight. Meanwhile, as the stars came out one by one, bright Celestia leading the way in the west, Ideth and Soccer Fan laid out their ducky sacks and, dog-tired from the day's ordeal, turned in for the night. Under the moons-less sky, their ducky sacks were tiny specks in the debris of the storm.

A week passed, and life on Krog Pad Island settled down. Soccer Fan played with his duppies, and the memory of the trilogy storm and its terrible cost faded. But soon, Soccer Fan lost interest in their usual games. After his heroic rescue of Iktae, the Krog Padders' shenanigans seemed rather silly. He knew all the games by heart, and he grew bored.

On the eighth night after the storm, he awoke with a

start just before dawn, not sure what had disturbed his slumber. He opened his eyes and sat up to look around, but no one was there. Lunera and Ru, both visible when he'd gone to bed, had slipped over the western horizon. The beach was eerily quiet. The island's usual chatty shorebirds had vacated the area during the storm and hadn't yet returned. There was no wind. The tide was out. The surf was far away, only a gentle gurgle now, like a distant memory.

A distant memory.

Soccer Fan looked up and stared deep into the heavens. The sky, raked clean of clouds by the trilogy storm, was inky black. Hundreds of stars, many very bright, a few vaguely red, sprinkled the heavens. The great constellation *Like Seahorse Is* curled its tail around Urth's pole star, *Always Up*. The Milky Way Galaxy sprawled majestically in the west, brighter than he'd ever seen it, impossibly close. For the first time, Soccer Fan noticed its central bulge, partially obscured by billowing clouds of interstellar dust. "Funny I never noticed it before, when I was out stars-gazing with my duppies," he thought. "But there it is, obvious as can be. There's no mistaking it."

Instinctively, he stood up. He suddenly felt himself drawn to the central bulge like a moth to a flame. "Ideth says Earth's on the other side of that bulge," he thought. "I miss it. *I miss Monterey. I miss my parents. I miss Mush. I even miss Alex. I miss them so much.*"

Weird. He hadn't thought about Earth in a very

long time. After all that had happened, it felt like years since he'd lived in Monterey. A lifetime ago. But now, an unexpected wave of homesickness washed over him. It was overwhelming.

Soccer Fan was drawn to the central
bulge like a moth to a flame...

"Why should I want to go back?" he asked himself. "Back to all the nagging? Back to the 'BLAH, BLAH, BLAH' lectures? Back to the comparisons to Alex? The dreaded Award Ceremonies?" But deep down inside, he knew why. He'd witnessed Iktae's joyful reunion with her distraught parents, who thought she was dead. Now, for the first time, he worried about his own parents. He wondered what they'd been going through. And Alex, too. What did they think had happened to him? Did they think he was dead, too? They must be frantic.

Soccer Fan eventually went back to sleep, but he

tossed and turned, and, as soon as Ideth began her usual early morning puttering, he came back to consciousness. As usual, her "hush hush" attempts *not* to wake him backfired, and soon he rose from his ducky sack and walked over to her.

She was sitting beside the fire, breathing on it to give it life. *Crackle pop.* She was dropping shellfish into the hot water one by one. *Plop, plop, plop.*

As Soccer Fan approached, she looked up.

"How do you feel?" she asked.

"Homesick," he replied.

"I'm not surprised. Earth is calling you home. Look at your fingers. They're almost back to their creamy brown, just like the rest of you. I noticed it last night. It's the sign that you've completed your mission."

Soccer Fan examined his fingers. The tips were no longer Psychedelic Grape. Instead, they were a limpid color somewhere between lavender and light brown. Wet Raisin, maybe.

Ideth continued. "The call of Earth is very strong at the end of a finding. It's the same way for every findling, every time. Of course, you can stay on Urth if you prefer. You're a renamed child, and it's your choice. 'No Findling Left Behind' is a general rule, but it's not set in stone. It's up to you."

"My mission was to save Iktae, wasn't it?" he asked, proudly.

She nodded. "Yes, I'm sure it was. And you carried it

out beautifully, I must say. I doubt any other boy would have done what you did, entering that awful crack and finding a way to rescue her. I'd certainly never have done it myself."

Soccer Fan sat down beside her, unsure what to do. He wanted to end his family's pain, the pain he was sure they were feeling. The agony, no doubt. But he was also worried about Iktae. What would happen to her if he went home?

Reading his mind, Ideth said, "I've thought about that and I've hatched a plan. My sister runs an orphanage on Cairntip, and I'm sure she'd be willing to care for the Krog Pad kids during the rainy season. 'Camp Monsoon,' we could call it. What do you think?"

Soccer Fan smiled. He was all in favor of it.

They sat in companionable silence for a couple of minutes. Then he said with a chuckle, "To tell you the truth, I'm kind of sick of this island. I like the Krog Padders, and I love Iktae, but honestly, they really are a bunch of overgrown babies, aren't they?"

Ideth laughed. "Indeed, they are. And I think you can do better than that. Don't you?"

Iktae was heartbroken when Soccer Fan told her he was leaving. She thought Ideth was forcing him to go, but he explained that it was his decision.

"I don't belong on Urth anymore," he said. "I belong on my own planet, far away. My parents must be missing me, wondering where I am. And I miss them, too."

He explained to her about the Monsoon Camp, but the idea didn't make much sense to her. She couldn't envision another trilogy storm coming.

Maybe she would one day. She was a remarkable Krog Padder, after all, and had grown so much, thanks to Soccer Fan. But not yet. Not quite yet.

"Thank goodness Ideth can see ahead and do something about these kids," he thought. "The Krog Padders are hopeless at protecting them."

Iktae ran off and told Shum about Soccer Fan's decision, and Shum told the others. Soon, the news about Ideth and Soccer Fan's imminent departure had spread like wildfire around the island, and all the Krog Padders came to the beach to see them off.

Iktae and Shum decided to follow them partway to the East End Paddling Station, but for the others it was a final good-bye.

"Happy sea!" they cried in unison, giving them hug after hug after hug until Ideth and Soccer Fan had received dozens of hugs apiece. The Krog Padders also hugged one another, as if unsure who was leaving whom. It was their version of "Bon Voyage!" and quite a send-off.

After he'd put on his mask and snorkel and adjusted it to fit "just right," Soccer Fan squatted down and hugged Iktae one last time. When he let her go, she kissed the front of his mask. Then she climbed onto her daddy's back and clutched his paddling tuft. It was an instinctive move. Soccer Fan had seen the Krog Padder kids do it countless times before. No one needed to instruct them how to hold on. They simply knew. They were born to it.

Ideth dragged the paddling buoy into the water, and soon she was afloat. After she was situated, the others followed her in. Soccer Fan reached for her tuft (left hand, he reminded himself, children paddle to the right), and repeated the paddling rules to himself. It had been months since he'd paddled with Ideth, but he remembered them, no problem.

The four of them took off, and for several miles, they swam side-by-side. *Thrust, thrust, float. Thrust, thrust, float.* Iktae didn't have a snorkel, but she didn't need one. Shum pushed her to the surface now and then for air, and she did fine. It was the first time Soccer Fan had witnessed an Urth parent paddle across the open ocean with a child, and their movements were coordinated flawlessly, like a well-rehearsed dance. In calm weather, with no storm surge, Iktae was perfectly safe.

After a while, though, Shum slowed down, and he and Iktae fell behind. At one point, Iktae realized what was happening and reached out with her free hand, batting Soccer's Fan's foot to say farewell one last time. He looked over his shoulder, smiled encouragingly, and met her eyes. She was weeping underwater (which Soccer Fan didn't think was possible), but when she smiled back through her water-tears and gave him a big thumbs up, he knew she'd be okay.

The next time he looked back, she was gone.

22

Elvia

deth and Soccer Fan reached the East End Paddling Station well before dark. This time, they were checked in by Mot, who, it turned out, was a bit scatterbrained.

He stared at his guest roster and said uncertainly, "Two berths, one uppy and one findling. Let's see... Is the Shark Room open? Yes, I think it is. I'll put you there. Dinner's included for findlings, and all that. You know the drill, Ideth."

Ideth and Soccer Fan made their way down to the Shark Room, but, when they arrived, they found that it was already occupied. From inside, they could hear a child, clearly upset, and the voice of a woman who was trying to soothe her.

The girl said, "I hate this room. It's scary."

"It's the room they assigned us, Elvia," the woman

replied, "and it's only for one night. Go choose a color for your feeling. There are lots of shades of fear. It's a juicy feeling if ever there was one."

Ideth pulled Soccer Fan away from the door.

"Clearly the wrong room," she whispered. "Let's go fix the mistake."

They climbed back up the ladder to the reception area and explained the error to Mot.

"Hmmm," he said, scratching his mop of stunning white hair. "Guess I already gave the Shark Room to that other uppy and her findling. Gets confusing when we have more than one set of you folks at the same time. But we still have the Mermaid Room."

He winked at Soccer Fan.

As he handed Ideth the key, he chuckled. "Not a good room for most boys."

Soccer Fan looked at Ideth and Ideth cleared her throat. They were both thinking the same thing.

"You know, Mot, I think the other uppy-findling pair might be willing to switch. Have they been here long?"

"Not long enough to settle in, if that's what you mean," he replied. "I'll go talk to them and see what they have to say."

Mot disappeared down the hole, and Soccer Fan looked through to the dining room. The same sign was there, announcing the dinner arrangements: "Dinner served promptly at seven. Loincloths respectfully suggested."

"Did you notice the owl?" Ideth asked with a smirk. "They've replaced it with a plastic gull-eating dolphin. Looks ridiculous."

Mot returned with a grin.

"You just made a girl very happy. She and her uppy are packing up now. As soon as they're moved out, you can move yourself in. Here's the key to the Shark Room."

Ideth and Soccer Fan waited a respectful ten minutes before returning to the belly of the hotel. The door to the Shark Room was cracked open, and inside it was empty.

Ideth stepped into the room and looked around. "Goodness! I can see why she didn't want to stay here. *Yuk!*"

Soccer Fan's reaction was completely different. He gaped with pleasure and wonder. There were murals of dozens of different kinds of sharks on the walls, swimming around. But the crowning glory of the room, and the one that Ideth's eyes were riveted on, was an enormous great purple, crushing a fisherman between its mighty jaws, guts and blood splashed everywhere.

"Wow! This is perfect. Look. The berths are inside the great purple's stomach!"

Ideth got busy unpacking, while Soccer Fan snooped around.

"I'd like the bottom berth, Ideth, if that's okay. It's got a pullout drawer beneath it filled with shark-themed jigsaw puzzles. There's a board that you can pull down to work on them in bed, and you can push it back up when you go to sleep. The puzzle stays in one piece until you're ready to work on it again. It's so cool!"

"Well, we got here early, so you'll have time for a puzzle. I just hope there aren't any pieces missing. I hate that."

While Soccer Fan chose a puzzle, Ideth wandered into the hallway and down to the Mermaid Room.

A bright-eyed Earth girl opened the door. She beamed at Ideth. "Are you the other uppy?"

"Yes, I am. And my guess is that you're the other findling. My name's Ideth, how about you?"

"I'm Elvia. Thanks for switching rooms with us."

Ideth noticed that Elvia was missing a tooth, her right-side canine. She smiled in recognition. "I remember how it feels to lose a tooth. You can run your tongue into the soft spot. It hurts but it feels kind of good at the same time."

The girl nodded. "Lacie says Urth children get *real* gold when they lose a tooth. She gave me a tooth pouch to wear around my neck tonight. If I put my tooth inside, the fairy will come during the night and swap it out."

She held out the small, bejeweled velvet bag for Ideth's inspection. Then she whispered, "I don't believe in the tooth fairy. I'm just pretending."

Ideth winked. "Just between us, then. You wouldn't want to miss out on real gold."

At that moment, Elvia's stately, knock-dead gorgeous

uppy appeared. She was a colleague and friend, but Ideth could never get over how queenly and beautiful she was. Her name was Lacie, and she wore an upscale, elegant version of sailing attire. It didn't look the least bit practical, but Ideth had to admit that the navy blouse set off the color of her almond-shaped, liquid blue eyes to great effect.

Lacie greeted her warmly.

"Ideth. What a lovely surprise. Are you on your way in or on your way out?"

"Out. And it was an unqualified success. Soccer Fan saved the life of a little girl named Iktae on Krog Pad Island. Isn't that something?"

"Well, I'm glad he completed his mission," Lacie said. "But honestly, I don't know how you survive camping on Krog Pad for weeks and weeks on end. No amenities. Makes me shiver."

It was a good-natured exchange. Lacie rather admired Ideth's ability to live close to the bone, and Ideth found Lacie's "high maintenance" lifestyle amusing.

"And you? Are you coming in or going out?" Ideth asked.

"We're coming in."

Ideth chuckled. "Well, you're off for another shopping expedition to Amdar Island, then. I'll bet you're looking forward to that."

"Indeed! I'm *Over the Moons!* And guess what? Asul gave me a clothing allowance this time."

Ideth had never heard of such a perk. "A what?"

Lacie laughed at her confusion. "You heard me right. A clothing allowance. He was desperate for an uppy, and I took advantage."

Ideth laughed along. Lacie was nothing if not enterprising. Asul was the head of the Uppy Council and widely known as a cheapskate.

Just then, Elvia piped up, "This room is *fantastic!* I'm so excited!"

Her attention refocused, Ideth, looked around with interest. Mermaids, swathed in pink and gold, bathed the walls. There was a grand vanity table with a huge mirror, a pretend mermaid cave, and a golden wand leaning against one wall.

Lacie said, "Oh, Elvia, excitement isn't just *excitement!* Can you color up your feeling?"

Elvia ran across the room and scooped up a colorful book. Then she flipped through the pages.

Settling on one page in particular, she cried, "Here's my feeling. It's *Fiesta*. Bright orange, like balloons at a party."

She grinned, ran over to the mermaid cave, and scooted inside.

Lacie and Ideth talked for a few more minutes, while Elvia continued her explorations of the Mermaid Room. Then they said their good-byes and Ideth returned to the Shark Room. Soccer Fan was putting together a particularly gory puzzle, depicting a sailor spearing a tiger shark through the eye.

"Good," she thought. "It has five hundred pieces. That should keep him busy until dinnertime and give me time for a nap. We'll be up early tomorrow."

Ideth climbed the ladder to the top berth, enjoying the luxury of knowing she wouldn't be banging her head on the berth above her. She looked out the porthole. It wasn't dark yet. The sea was green and gold in the filtered sunlight. Several colorful reef fish darted past, showing off their yellows and bright blues.

She sighed and let her body completely relax into the gentle rocking rhythm of the station. It was so satisfying to finish another finding. Now she'd return home, spend a few days cleaning and organizing her cave (first things first!), and then sink into the bliss of "repositioning," an uppy's version of vacation.

The dining room was packed. Soccer Fan and Ideth got there early. Their section of the table was already full by the time Elvia and Lacie arrived. The guests were chattering and the band was playing, but the moment Lacie entered, the room fell quiet. All eyes were on her.

"Oh, for pity's sake," Ideth thought. "A formal evening gown, Lacie? Really? Like as not, you'll tear it to shreds. This is a paddling station, not a cruising submarine!"

Everyone gawked as stately Lacie, her findling in tow, glided to two open seats. A man leapt up and pulled out her chair, pushing away another who'd jumped up to do the same.

Soccer Fan whispered, "Is that the other uppy?"

Ideth turned to him and nodded. Soccer Fan's mouth was agape.

"Wow," he muttered. "She's unbelievable."

Ideth laughed. "You've no idea."

Soccer Fan was curious about Lacie's findling, but Elvia was largely hidden from view. At one point, however, he locked eyes with her and gave her an encouraging smile. He knew what it was like to be new to Urth, before you knew the ropes.

"Lucky it's a trilogy," he thought. "No moons-shock for her."

When Soccer Fan and Ideth got back to the Shark Room, it was dark outside. Soccer Fan was only thirty pieces short of completing his puzzle, and he eagerly asked Ideth to help him finish.

"You go ahead," she said. "I think I'm going to hit the ducky sack early."

With a glint in his eye, he pleaded "Pleeeze? I could really use your help."

Ideth relented and chipped in, but when they got to the last piece, they couldn't find it.

"Is it on the floor?" Soccer Fan asked, leaning over and inspecting beneath the berth. Ideth looked under the puzzle box and slid her hand between the bedding and the berth board. Nothing.

"Oh, I *hate* this," she muttered. "I always seem to get the puzzles with pieces missing. And darned if it isn't just *one* piece this time. So frustrating!"

Soccer Fan grinned, reached under his pillow, and pulled out the final piece. "Gotcha!" he said, as he slipped it into place.

It was the shark's pierced, bloody eye.

23

The Returning

Before they geared up and set out the next morning, Ideth prepared Soccer Fan for what to expect. "A returning is much simpler than a finding. It takes far less time. You'll be back in Monterey, hugging your parents, before you know it."

Soccer Fan was excited, but also sad. He wanted to take Ideth with him.

"You could come home with me," he offered. "I wish you would."

"I'd love to," Ideth said, "but findings just don't work that way. It's bittersweet, but our time together is over. We'll be apart forever but you'll be in my heart when I wake every morning and again in my heart when I go to sleep every night. We're linked that way, and always will be."

Soccer Fan fought back tears, but bravely soldiered on. "So, what happens now? Where do we go?"

"Returning Island. Half a day's paddle. The buoy is stocked, sealed, and ready to go. We can snack along the way if we get desperate. I saved some cake from dinner."

Soccer Fan remembered their lunch in the ocean during his first paddle. He hoped to avoid a repeat performance of that watery experience. It was hard to believe that his journey "in" had been only six months before. It seemed like a lifetime. Now he was on his way "out."

He wondered what he would say to his parents when he got home. "How will I tell them about Urth? How can I possibly explain? They'll think I've gone nuts and put me in a mental hospital."

He pictured himself in a straight-jacket, being led away. The doctor would say, "Kid's gone nuts. Totally bonkers. Off the rails. Says he's been on the other side of the galaxy all these months, with purple people."

Ideth laughed. "Those things will take care of themselves," she said. "Trust me. Am I right, or am I right?"

It was a lovely paddle. The *thrust, thrust, float* was familiar and soothing. The tingling along his skin, when Ideth navigated, was oddly comforting. The sea creatures were beautiful. Two huge yellow lobsters, fiercely protecting their turf, waved their antennae at Soccer Fan. A friendly red octopus, no bigger than a cat, brushed his leg, as if saying "Hi there, big fella." He didn't see a shark this time, which rather disappointed him, and he didn't spot a dodecopus. Not even one. Oh, well. He still enjoyed a delightful fantasy of meeting one face to face and slicing it to death with a mighty sword. In his mind, the dodecopus' blood was the color of black ink and heavier than seawater. It would slowly sink to the ocean floor, along with the body parts of its owner.

The weather was calm most of the way. It only kicked up at the very end. Every now and then, Ideth surfaced to breathe and they looked around. Just before noon, they surfaced for the last time.

"There!" Ideth said, pointing to a low island covered with trees. "That's Returning Island. No fruit there, but you won't be on the island long enough to get hungry."

The tide was rising. They rode a large swell in, and it delivered them to a slender beach riddled with small stones. A few shore birds pecked about, but there were no turtles. Wet and tired, they crawled onto the land.

Soccer Fan offered to help Ideth drag her buoy onto the beach, but she said there was no need.

"As soon as I see you off, I'll be heading back to Cairntip. Uppies aren't supposed to linger at a returning. It's bad luck. I'll paddle to the West End Paddling Station this evening, and, if all goes well, I'll arrive in time for dinner."

She told him a bit about the station. She preferred the Nautilus Room to all others. "Built like a maze.

You have to crawl through a series of complicated iridescent tunnels to reach the berth." Then she added, "Time to remove your wetsuit and get dressed in your Earth clothes."

Soccer Fan retrieved his clothes from the buoy and changed, while Ideth looked the other way. When he was done, he carefully rolled his loincloth and wetsuit, military style, and placed them on the rocks, beside his mask and snorkel. It was the last time he'd see them.

When he was done, Ideth looked him up and down with approval.

"Those clothes are too small for you now. You've grown at least an inch since you arrived. Your muscles are amazing. And look at that mane of hair you have now. Looks so grown up."

Soccer Fan smiled at the compliment. His hair was below his shoulders, and he liked it that way.

"I love you, Ideth. Not the way I love my mother, but in another, special way. If I could have two mothers, I'd choose you as my second."

Ideth smiled. "I'll always be your Urth mother, Soccer Fan. A boy can never have too many mothers. And like I said, I'll take care of Iktae and the others. Don't you worry."

Soccer Fan eyes grew wet. He had a hard time thinking about Iktae without tearing up.

"What's going to become of her?" he asked.

"Well, for one thing, she'll have a life, thanks to

you," Ideth said. "She'll romp in the present moment, just like all her people. But I'll drop off books for her now and then. Wouldn't want her reading to get rusty. She enjoys it so."

"I don't think she'll stay on Krog Pad forever," Frankie said, deep in thought. "I think she'll go to Cairntip and save a kid from his ambitious, pushy parents."

Ideth nodded, amazed at Frankie's insight. "Ha!" she said, "Why I believe you're right. You saved her, and now she'll pay the favor forward, to another child, in her own, very special way."

Soccer Fan contemplated this for a moment before Ideth continued, "One thing I know for sure is that she'll never be a worrier. Folks who fret too much could learn a thing or two from your duppies. They're so happy and carefree."

"Mom and dad are always worrying about me," Soccer Fan said." They say I'll end up in a gutter."

Ideth laughed. "As I see it, you have three choices, and not one of them involves a gutter. You can twist yourself into someone else to please your parents, you can listen to their 'BLAH BLAH BLAH' lectures until you're forty, or you can find a way to use your wonderful gift of *Fantasy* to make a living and get out from under their thumbs."

The idea of morphing himself into a kid like Alex had no appeal, and the prospect of listening to his parents' lectures until he was an old man made him wince.

"There are plenty of people with the gift of *Fantasy* who support themselves doing what they love," Ideth continued. "They play in dreamland most of the time, but they crawl out of their imaginations and share their fantasies now and then. And they get paid for it."

Soccer Fan caught on. "Writers?"

"And artists. You bet. Fantasy's a big genre, and you're a natural."

Soccer Fan grew excited. He'd never considered this possibility.

"You mean I don't have to be a doctor or lawyer or engineer?" he asked.

"Absolutely not," Ideth assured him. "And I'll tell you what, Frankie Soccer Fan Russo. I'll march all the way across the galaxy and rap your knuckles if you do!"

Ideth and Soccer Fan spontaneously reached out and hugged one another.

"Well done, findling. You did great. Now go into the forest and the returning will happen all by itself."

Soccer Fan walked to the edge the forest, where a faint trail disappeared into the shady interior. He looked back one last time. His final image of Ideth was of her waving to him from the beach, the buoy and his abandoned paddling gear beside her. She looked happy for him.

He didn't know what to do. Ideth had given him no instructions. He had no food, no water, no ducky sack.

He followed the trail in. The forest closed behind him and the sounds of the beach faded away.

He recalled how he'd felt in the Finding Forest when he'd first arrived. Happy, homey, peaceful. Returning Island was different. Rather than drawing him in, it seemed to be pushing him out. A profound sense of unease settled over him. He didn't belong in the Returning Forest. Not for long. He needed to go home.

The Returning Trees were tall and straight. He stopped beside one of the loftiest and looked up. It was as tall as the massive redwoods he'd seen in Sequoia National Park on a family vacation.

The side branches of the trees were horizontal and only a couple of feet apart. They were thick and looked strong. They offered a ladder upwards, to the sky.

There was no question. He was going to climb the tree. Before his adventure on Urth, he would never have attempted it. But now he knew he could do it, even if his acrophobia kicked in.

Branch after branch, he made his way up, ever closer to the bright, promising, blue patches peeking through the canopy high above. He didn't pretend he was King of the Purple Fruit Monkeys. He was too keen to leave the forest to waste time doing that. Instead, he focused on fantasies about what he'd do when he got home.

He imagined himself deftly climbing up the experts' wall at the Just Hangin' Out Rock Gym, topping out while an admiring crowd watched and hooted encouragement

from below. He'd do it in his bare feet, with no rope, no chalk bag, and no little orange pills to help dampen his acrophobia. His parents would be amazed. Alex would be dumbfounded.

He fantasized cooking dinner for the entire neighborhood on his first night home, whipping up pancakes with strawberry jam and hot chocolate, over a campfire in the backyard. Everyone would beg for second and third helpings, thunderstruck by his skills as a chef. Soon, he'd have his own cooking show on TV, Frankie's Feasts, and make a million bucks.

He imagined scooping a heap of forbidden food into Mush's doggie dish: oysters fresh from the shell. Mush would gobble them up immediately, with unbridled enthusiasm. *Mush.* His very own Krog Padder on Earth to feed as he pleased without any interference from his parents.

When he reached the top of the canopy, the view took his breath away. Returning Island, it turned out, was almost perfectly round. From above, the Returning Trees were silver and seemed to be holding hands, swaying together in the gusty wind, as if waving good-bye.

Soccer Fan looked over his shoulder at the expansive panorama, now fully in view. The sun was overhead, and Lunera, at first quarter, was rising in the east. The sea stretched unbroken in all directions, punctuated only by another low-lying island nearby, glinting purple in the sun like a sparkling, amethyst jewel.

"It's Finding Island!" he realized, a bit lightheaded now. "If only I had my cell phone, I'd take a photo for mom."

It was Soccer Fan's final thought on Urth, and I think we can agree it was a generous one. But it came and went quickly, for he was suddenly drawn back home, never to return.

Tingle! Zap! Siphon! Noodle! Freeze! Gasp! Swell!

In the blink of an eye, the Returning Forest had vanished and Soccer Fan was crossing the airless void of outer space again, on a journey that would liberate his anguished family from their terrible loss and poor Jimmy Albini from a life in prison.

A galaxy of suns, billions of them with planets like Earth and Urth, streaked past in only twenty-eight seconds. "If only I could visit them all one day!" he thought briefly, as he whizzed along.

And then, with a crushing deceleration and an unceremonious little plop, Frankie (no longer Soccer Fan) found himself breathless and wide-eyed, lying on his bed in Monterey, staring up at the crack in the ceiling that had started his adventure so many months before.

24

Homecoming

O fficer Morgan was sitting at the desk in his small office at the police station. It had a tiny window that was broken in three places, the result of an accident years before, when some stupid juvenile delinquents had slammed into the building with a car. The glass had never been replaced, and it reminded him, every time he happened to see it, of how little money his department had to spend. If he'd chosen a different line of work—been a stockbroker, perhaps—he might now own a fine house by the sea. Instead, he lived with his unhappy wife in a modest cottage two blocks away.

It was a slow day. Monterey had little crime, and, when it did, the offenses were usually minor, requiring more paperwork than actual policing. He was buried under a pile of late reports. He had four large binders open on his desk, stacks of disorganized papers under them, a desk calendar below that, and, at the very bottom, a squashed cinnamon roll that he'd bought for breakfast more than three months earlier. He'd put it down on his desk when he'd been called into his boss' office for a meeting (having to do with late paperwork), and he'd forgotten all about it. Now, it was in the early stages of fossilization.

Officer Morgan was typing on his computer and drinking his third cup of coffee for the morning, when his cell phone rang.

A breathless, excited voice spoke to him from the other end of the line.

"Officer Morgan, FRANKIE'S HOME!" Evelyn Russo cried in an ecstatic voice. "He walked into the kitchen while I was making lunch. Roberto and I can't believe it, but it's true! We're overjoyed! You need to get over here, right now!"

Officer Morgan knew Mrs. Russo's voice instantly, and the hairs on his arms and the back of neck stood on end.

Leaping up and upsetting his coffee, he cried, "What? What the heck are you saying?"

"I'm telling you. FRANKIE IS HOME! He's safe. I don't know how it happened, but he's home."

"We'll be right there!" Officer Morgan cried, dropping his cell phone in disbelief.

He sprinted out of his office into the break room, where several other police officers were making coffee

Frankie's parents were overjoyed…

and getting ready for what they thought was going to be another dull day, too.

"Frankie Russo has been found!" he shouted. "He's alive! I just got a call from his mother. He's at their house!"

There was a stunned silence.

"Are you sure?" asked one of the officers, coming out of her chair in surprise.

"I haven't seen him yet myself, to confirm, but unless his mother's gone crazy, yes. He wasn't murdered after all."

The station became a flurry of activity. Everyone had to be told, a team of officers needed to be dispatched to the Russo home, and someone had to contact Social Services to get a child trauma psychologist involved. It wouldn't be long before the media would get a whiff of the story and then all heck would break loose.

They decided not to turn on their sirens. They didn't want to attract any more attention than absolutely necessary. Nevertheless, the arrival of three police cars and an ambulance aroused the curiosity of the Russo's neighbors. Amber Duncan, who lived two doors down, walked outside to see what all the fuss was about.

Soon, many of the Russo's neighbors had wandered into the street, too, and were talking to one another, speculating about what was happening. Within twenty minutes of the officers' arrival, one of them had called Channel 12.

Frankie was in remarkably good shape for a boy who'd supposedly been abducted and murdered. His clothes were too small for him and rather frayed, but they also appeared to have been carefully mended in several places. His hair was long, but not dirty. He was badly sunburned and his shoulder was badly bruised, but, all told, he was physically fine.

His mental state was excellent, too. When the officers walked in the door, Frankie was in good spirits. Mush was racing around the house, leaping and barking with excitement, and Frankie was right behind him, laughing and trying to catch his tail.

No one asked Frankie what had happened. Not yet. The child psychologist was firm about that.

She told his family, "He'll give us the story in his own time. Right now, he needs to be looked over by the paramedics to make sure he's okay, and then they'll transport him to the hospital for a more thorough examination. As long as he's in no imminent danger, we'll release him to you in a few hours. You can stay with him the entire time. I know you won't want him out of your sight."

They all nodded, tears of joy streaming down their faces. They'd been crying ever since Frankie had miraculously returned, overcome with emotion.

The psychologist also prepared them for what was about to happen in their lives.

"You've been in the eyes of the media before, so you know what it's like. They'll be hounding you from the moment this gets out. I suggest you let the police do the talking on your behalf, and Frankie mustn't be allowed to talk to them at all. This is an ongoing criminal investigation and it's important that he talks only to you and the police."

Then she squatted down to look Alex directly in the eyes. "You may be excited and want to text your friends and put this up on social media, but you can't do that until we get this sorted out. Okay? I need your word on that, little buddy."

Alex nodded solemnly, looking up at his parents with wide eyes.

"It'll be okay," said his father, ruffling his hair. "We'll help you through this."

It was several hours before they got home from the hospital, and Frankie slept between his ecstatic parents that night, something he hadn't done since he was a very young child. But it felt so wonderful to have them on both sides, snuggling him and breaking out in sobs of gratitude every minute or two, that he wouldn't have wanted to be anywhere else. Alex joined them, curling up at Frankie's feet.

Even Frankie's grandmother eventually joined the communal hug, hopping into bed with them around midnight.

"You know," she said, "I feel twenty years younger. I always knew everything would be all right."

Over the ensuing three weeks, the police interviewed Frankie again and again. Each new cop who took a statement wanted to hear the story from "square one," as if they'd stumble onto something new, or catch him in a lie.

But Frankie told the same story every time.

I was sucked thorough a crack in my bedroom ceiling to a distant planet called Urth, on the other side of the galaxy. I had moons-shock at first, but then I met Ideth, who made everything okay. She's a purple woman with webbed feet and a layer of blubber around her middle, and she told me I have the gift of Fantasy. Then she paddled me to an underwater hotel where I renamed myself Soccer Fan, using Francesco, not Frankie. On Krog Pad Island, I lived in a cave and met Iktae. It was my mission to save her, 'cause they have these horrible storms at syzygies and the Krog Padders don't prepare. Urth has two moons, you see...

Eventually, the cops stopped taking notes. Quietly, behind shut doors, they closed his case.

"Kid's gone nuts," the head of the Monterey Police Department said sadly, shaking his head. "Totally bonkers. Off the rails. Says he's been on the other side of the galaxy all these months, with purple people."

"Yup, yup, Boss," Officer Morgan agreed. "Frankie has the gift of *Fantasy*, all right, ha, ha! I guess we'll just have to live with *not knowing what happened*. Let's hope it doesn't eat us alive inside."

25

Jimmy Albini Writes a Book

What did it *feel* like when you knew you were going to be released?" asked Maria Thomson, the tanned, toothy, and snappily attired host of Good Day Monterey. Her long legs were crossed and disappeared seamlessly into shoes made of fine Italian leather that were the same color as her flawless skin.

Jimmy, a microphone clipped to his lapel, smiled.

"It felt good," he said simply.

Maria expected him to elaborate, but he didn't. An awkward silence ensued.

Jimmy was a man of few words, which made him a terrible guest on a talk show. "This will be difficult," she thought. "I need to draw him out."

Maria quickly swooped in to fill the auditory vacuum.

"I'm sure you must have felt better than just good," she suggested, smiling at him encouragingly. "You were thrilled, no doubt."

The camera swung from her to Jimmy. "Yes," said Jimmy.

Another silence.

Maria leaned forward. "What was the first thing you did when you got back home? I'll bet you hugged your family pretty hard."

Jimmy winced. Actually, the first thing he'd done was to go to the bathroom. But he couldn't say that on the air. And he didn't have a family, so that hardly applied.

More silence.

Maria cast a sympathetic glance to the camera. "Well," she said, "maybe you'd like to keep those precious moments to yourself, Jimmy. I think I would in your position."

Maria changed her approach, and Jimmy was relieved. "So, what's next?" she asked brightly.

"A book," Jimmy said. He'd had publishers hounding him ever since he'd been released from prison and had multiple offers of deals linked to dollar figures so high that he had trouble comprehending them.

Maria cried brightly, "A book! Wow, Jimmy, that's fantastic. I'm sure our listeners would *love* to hear your story. An upstanding citizen accused of a horrible crime that he didn't commit… languishing in jail for months

awaiting trial... convicted... now completely exoner-
ated..." Her eyebrows shot upward. "If that's not bestseller material, I don't know what is!"

Jimmy squirmed. Before his imprisonment, he'd
hardly been an upstanding citizen. Maria was refram-
ing his life to fit her viewers' preferred fantasy of him.
He'd found that the media were fond of doing that; rec-
reating a person's life to serve their purpose, running
roughshod over the complicated truth to make money.

He'd been the center of attention for weeks now
and most of it was wonderful. Bob Grebes had offered
him his old job back, with a raise, telling the press that
Jimmy was the best worker he'd ever had. Sara and her
sisters had cleaned his apartment until it shone, hung
curtains, and then thrown him a huge party.

He'd gotten mail from all over the country and most
of it sat, unopened, beside his mail box. The outpouring
of sympathy and congratulations was overwhelming.
His story had captivated the nation.

Frankie's family had apologized so many times that
Jimmy felt embarrassed. The prosecutor had made
several public appearances to admit his wrongdoing.
He'd been overzealous, he admitted. The district attorney's office, he promised, would be more careful in the
future. The blood on the towel in the Russo kitchen was
easily explained, and he felt sheepish.

But the media were simply a pain. Jimmy could see
right through their tactics and found them shameful.

He'd agreed to the interview with Maria just to get her off his back.

Maria began again. "Do you have a title for your book yet? Our listeners will want to know."

Jimmy replied simply, *"The Art of Roofing."*

The title wasn't at all what Maria had expected, and she frowned. Why would a man like Jimmy Albini write a book about roofing when he could write one about his terrible ordeal and make a fortune? Jimmy saw the look of disappointment on her face, but he didn't care. His book wouldn't be written for people like Maria, so what did it matter? He already had the chapters laid out in his mind.

After the show was over, Jimmy was escorted to the front door of the studio by a lovely young woman who whispered, "You did great in there. Maria is such an exploitative prig."

Jimmy laughed and they talked for several more minutes in front of the studio. Lila was an artist and was only working at the studio to save up enough money to take a year off.

"I want to paint," she said. "It's all I ever do in my free time, so I figure I should take a shot at making it my living. But I need to build up a bigger portfolio."

Jimmy told her about his job as a roofer and explained that carpentry was a kind of art as well.

"You look at the job and you think, 'How can I make this roof last longer? How can I make sure it doesn't keep leaking?' There are so many slip-shod companies out there. They use cheap materials and cut corners all over the place. We don't do that at Bob's Roofing. We like to do things right."

"Yes, I do, too," Lila thought to herself. "I like this guy." They spoke for a few more minutes, and then a very odd thing happened. Jimmy asked Lila out on a date, and she accepted. A few years later, when they were married and had a daughter on the way, Jimmy laughed at how scared he'd once been of women.

He told Lila, "I used to think I wasn't worth much, but then—I don't know why—something shifted. It's like I suddenly woke up from a bad dream. When I looked in the mirror, I didn't think I was useless and couldn't do anything right. I saw a man who'd survived a terrible childhood and found a way past it. I saw a man I could respect."

The Art of Roofing sold very well, partly because Jimmy's exoneration had made him a celebrity, and partly because it wasn't just about roofing.

"When you find a leak, try to figure out what caused it," he wrote on page twenty-two, "not just how to fix it. Because if you don't address the cause, it will leak again."

Jimmy might have been talking about his own life, or the lives of so many of the other young people he'd known in prison. If a judge had taken the time to find out why they committed crimes, not just how to punish them, they might have escaped the system, like he had. He was lucky that a judge had given him a second chance at age nineteen, allowing him to fix the leak in his own life for good.

But King Pin, and many others like him, would spend their lives locked away, their potential wasted. Maybe one of them could have mastered a craft like Jimmy had, or even written a bestseller that held the number one position on the *New York Times* bestseller list for three weeks in a row. Instead, a young man with the gift of *A Free Spirit* might spend his days doing laundry and trading contraband for cigarettes, and a teenage girl with the gift of *Taking Care of Others* might hide out in her prison cell, afraid to reach out and shower her love on anyone, lest they turn on her.

Jimmy also had hidden advice for people who'd been traumatized as children and needed help to move on with their lives.

"Sometimes, a roof is so damaged that you need to start over," he wrote. "And that's okay. The beauty of being your own carpenter is that you get to create your roof exactly as you want it. Don't leave a nail unhammered. Don't leave a gap unsealed. If you do things right, your roof will last a lifetime, and no matter what happens, you'll be okay."

26

The Forgetting

We're nearly at the end of this story, as you've probably figured out because this is the last chapter.

But there's one important, very important, thing I have left to tell you.

If you're ever in Monterey and run into Frankie, you won't be able to ask him about his adventure on Urth. Nor will you be able to ask his parents, or Alex, or Jimmy Albini, or Officer Morgan, about the six months that Frankie was missing. You see, something very odd happens soon after a child returns from Urth. He forgets all about it. And his parents forget about their trauma and pain, and everyone else forgets about their role in what happened.

Everyone forgets, but everyone's been changed forever, too.

Jimmy Albini won't be able to recall what inspired him to write *The Art of Roofing*, but he'll build up a nice nest egg from the sales. Then he'll use the money to start a company of his own, called Second Chance Roofing. True to his gift of *Doing Things Right*, he'll sit on the board of a non-profit organization that helps troubled teenagers get a leg up, offering them jobs at his company without any incentive from the government.

One of Jimmy's young parolees, a kid named Brad, will discover that he *Likes Bats,* and one day find a cure for rabies that wins him the Nobel Prize. Another, a shy African American girl whose nose was broken three times by her abusive foster mother, will follow her gift of *Dreaming Big Dreams* and invent a solar fuel cell that solves the world's energy crisis and prevents a Great Melt from occurring on Earth.

Alex's experience with losing Frankie will make him a bit more cautious than he was before, and it will save his life one icy winter's night, when he'll 'round a corner in his car more slowly than he would have otherwise, missing the truck with the drunk driver, who will wander into the wrong lane.

Officer Morgan, who witnessed the miraculous recovery of a child who'd been missing for half a year, will realize there's more to life than staying in a secure job that makes a person unhappy. He'll retire from the police force early and move back to his home town in upstate New York, where he and his wife will reconnect and begin to enjoy each other's company for the first time in years.

August Slepe will abandon practicing law, inspired to sell mattresses for a living instead, a good fit for a man with the gift of *Snooze,* who never should have been an attorney.

Stella Knight will resign from her position at the crime lab to pursue a doctorate in ecology, using her scientific prowess to save an endangered species of sea otter. She'll be surprised by her decision, but never look back, and when she reads about an arrest in the paper, she'll always keep an open mind and wonder if the suspect is innocent.

The prosecutor will move on, too, returning to his Vietnamese roots. During a visit to the country of his forebears, he'll be inspired to take vows as a Buddhist monk, turning his clever mind to more lofty pursuits in his work as a prison chaplain.

Frankie's parents will change as well, no longer viewing their son as lazy and self-absorbed. They won't insist that he become a doctor or lawyer or engineer. They'll still badger him about his homework now and then, and sometimes his mother will ask him to stop twiddling with his pencil. But they won't compare him to Alex, and they won't insist that he kick a soccer ball harder and farther than his friends, unless he wants to.

They won't know why their attitude toward him has softened, nor why one day, at his request, they withdraw him from Hatfield Elementary and enroll him in the Monterey School for the Arts.

As for Frankie, he'll thrive, emerging from his education as an author of children's books, a prodigious writer whose imagination is heralded as extraordinary. He'll earn a living with his writing, but his chosen path won't always be easy. Sometimes he'll get writer's block and feel like giving up. But thinking ahead to the next paycheck, which won't come if he doesn't "hop to," he'll laugh and tell himself: "C'mon Frankie, I know you can finish writing this novel. Just apply yourself a little harder. Stop fiddling with your pencil. It doesn't *always* have to be a sword."

One day, he'll receive a fan letter from an unexpected source: a young man in a distant country. "One of my great-aunts bought me your book, and I read it on my cell phone while I was herding my goats. You have the same name that I do. Would you like to be pen pals?"

Eventually, Frankie will marry Katie, a shy librarian whose fondness for books entrances him, and they'll adopt a happy-go-lucky dog and name him Shum. Frankie won't know why he insists on giving the dog such a strange name. Nor will he understand why he prefers to drive Shum several miles out of his way, to the Monterey Beach Dog Park, rather than exercising him closer to home. Sometimes he'll simply watch his dog rapturously playing in the waves, but often he'll join him in his doggy frolicking. And when he does, he'll sport a joyous, goofy grin and shout "Happy be!" for no reason, under the bright Monterey sun.

THE END

Glossary and Pronunciation Guide

Alex Russo: Frankie Russo's "perfect" younger brother.

Amdar: A stormy resort island in Urth's southern ocean, where uppies take findlings with the gift of *Passion*.

Anagram: A word, phrase or name formed by rearranging the letters of another, such as cinema, formed from iceman.

August Slepe: Jimmy Oscar Albini's deadbeat, incompetent defense attorney.

Boatman: A person (not necessarily a man) who watches for flares sent up by uppies who have found their findlings and are ready to leave Finding Island.

Bob's Roofing: The business where Jimmy Oscar Albini was working when he was arrested for Frankie's abduction and murder.

Bob Grebes: Owner of Bob's Roofing who takes a chance and hires Jimmy Oscar Albini.

Cairntip Island: The largest island on Urth. The center of trade and commerce and Ideth's home.

Celestia: A planet similar to Venus that shines brightly in Urth's morning or evening skies. It has three moons.

Chatterboxes: Cell phone-like devices that Urth people used for communication before the Great Melt.

CODIS: The United States' national database of DNA profiles from known criminals that can be used to identify the perpetrator of a crime.

Dodecopus: A fierce sea monster, native to Urth's oceans, that boasts twelve enormous tentacles.

***Doing Things Right*:** The inclination to produce work of the highest quality. Jimmy Albini's gift.

Ducky sack: A very comfortable sleeping bag stuffed with the feathers of a Cairntip doow duck.

Duppies: Urth people who play a role in a findling's Urth adventure.

Elvia (El-vee-uh): A findling with the gift of *Passion*. Elvia is about to start her Urth adventure while Frankie Russo is finishing his.

East End Paddling Station: An underwater hotel halfway between Finding Island and Krog Pad Island. Sometimes called "The East Ender" for short.

Echolocation: A navigation system used by Urth people while paddling. It involves emitting sound waves and detecting their echoes to determine where objects are in deep and murky waters.

Evelyn Russo: Frankie Russo's well-meaning but nagging "helicopter mom."

Fantasy: The faculty or activity of imagining things, especially things that are impossible or improbable. Frankie's gift.

Finding: Either the actual "finding" of an Earth child by his uppy, or, more generally, the duration, from beginning to end, of a findling's adventure on Urth.

Finding Island: The island where uppies go to find their findlings. Finding Island is covered with Finding Trees bearing tasteless Finding Fruit.

Findling: An Earth child who's drawn to Urth to carry out an important mission.

Flare: A type of pyrotechnic (firework) that produces a brilliant light or intense heat without an explosion. On Urth, flares are used as a form of communication over long distances, especially at sea.

Francesco "Frankie" Russo: A ten-year-old Earth boy with the gift of *Fantasy*. He is the protagonist of the story.

Gift: A natural strength or inclination. Every person has one. Gifts can be expressed as nouns (e.g., *Tall Tales, Big Thoughts, Many Feelings*) or as verbs (*Telling Tall Tales, Thinking Big Thoughts, Having Many Feelings*), depending on the context.

The Great Melt: A catastrophic event on Urth when the ice cap glaciers melted, the sea levels rose, and the planet lost all its great continents. The Great Melt happened very quickly and reduced Urth's landmasses to a set of widely distributed islands.

Ideth: Grandmotherly-like Urth woman who is Frankie Russo's uppy.

Iktae: Shum's shy and book-loving young daughter.

Jimmy Oscar Albini: Innocent man accused of Frankie Russo's abduction and murder.

King Pin: The leader of Jimmy Oscar Albini's gang who appreciates Jimmy's gift of *Doing Things Right*. After Jimmy gets out of the gang and is living a lonely life, he names his cat after him.

Krog Pad Island: Island where uppies take children with the gift of *Fantasy*.

Krog Padders: The goofy, fun-loving residents of Krog Pad Island.

Krog Pad dialect: An abbreviated form of English spoken by Krog Padders.

Lacie: Elvia's gorgeous and resourceful uppy.

Laup: A boatman who meets Frankie Russo and Ideth on Finding Island and stocks them for their trip to Krog Pad Island.

Light year: The distance light travels in one year. It is nearly six trillion miles.

Lila: The delightful young assistant of Maria Thomson, whom Jimmy Albini eventually marries.

Lunera: The larger and brighter of Urth's two moons.

Maria Thomson: A manipulative reporter who tries to sensationalize Jimmy Oscar Albini's unjust incarceration.

Moons-light: The light cast by two moons.

Moons-shadow: A shadow, typically fuzzy, created by the light of two moons.

Moons-shock: A terrifying reaction to seeing Urth's two moons for the first time. It's especially acute when both moons are full and a findling hasn't yet met his uppy.

Mush: The good-natured Russo family dog.

Neap tides: Mild, almost motionless tides that occur when Urth's moons and sun balance one another's pulls on the planet.

Officer Morgan: Insensitive police officer leading the investigation into Frankie Russo's mysterious disappearance.

Paddle-saddlers: Fast-swimming Urth people who carry messages and mail between islands.

Paddling: Swimming. Urth people are adapted to life by the ocean and can paddle long distances with minimal effort. Adults can echolocate to navigate in murky or deep waters and can hold their breaths for up to half an hour.

Pot nut butter: A culinary delicacy, popular on Urth, that's prepared from the ground-up pellets of pot nut owls.

Prosecutor: An attorney tasked with obtaining convictions of suspects charged with crimes.

***Reading Minds*:** The ability to eavesdrop on the thoughts and daydreams of others. Ideth's gift.

Rename: An anagram of a child's name. Urth children rename themselves around the age of ten and have more control over their lives afterwards. Findlings also choose a rename during their findings.

Renaming letters: Small wooden squares, each with a letter, much like Scrabble pieces without the numbers. They're used by children to rename themselves.

Returning Island: The island where uppies take their findlings when they are ready to return to Earth.

Roberto Russo: Frankie Russo's well-meaning but nagging "helicopter dad."

Ru: The smaller and dimmer of Urth's two moons.

Sara: A kind young woman who rejects Jimmy Oscar Albini's invitation for a date.

Shum: One of Frankie Russo's loveable duppies. Shum's people live on Krog Pad Island.

Soccer Fan: Frankie's rename. (Based on his full first name, Francesco.)

Spaghetti willows: Graceful, delicate trees, native to Urth, that produce a fragrant, expensive oil used in cooking.

Stars-gazing: Looking at stars. On Urth, stars-gazing is best done during trilogies, when both moons are new and it's dark all night long.

Stella Knight: The prim DNA expert who provides incriminating testimony at Jimmy Oscar Albini's trial.

Stripe: A "degree" earned by an uppy that qualifies him/her to find an Earth child.

System: The criminal justice system.

Syzygy (<u>Sizz</u>-uh-gee): An astronomical event when Urth and its two moons are lined up in a straight line. At a harvest syzygy, both moons are full. At a trilogy, both moons are new. Urth's tides are extreme during syzygies.

Tales by Moons-light: Stories from before the Great Melt: A beloved book of fairy tales read by Urth children.

***The Art of Roofing*:** The best-selling book that Jimmy Oscar Albini writes after he is freed from prison.

***The Good Urth*:** A cookbook.

Trilogy: A syzygy in which Urth's two moons and its sun are lined up on the same side of the planet. The moons are both new during a trilogy and the nights are very dark and filled with stars, perfect for stars-gazing all night long.

Uppies: Urth people who find findlings and guide them on their adventures.

Uppy Academy: An elite school where uppies earn their stripes.

Uppy Council: Governing body that oversees the activities of uppies.

Urth ("Yearth"): An Earth-like planet on the other side of the Milky Way galaxy. Earth children are sometimes drawn there by a mysterious force.

Urth person: Human-like beings who live on Urth. They have lavender skin, webbed feet, and a layer of indigo blubber around their midsections.

Watler: A trader that Frankie and Ideth meet at the East End Paddling Station.

Win-nins: Golden nuts composed of a hard shell and a seed. When roasted and ground to a powder, they taste like chocolate.

Synopsis of Tales by Moons-light: Stories from before the Great Melt

At exactly 14:00 hours Universal Mean Time on February 5, 1961, twelve-year-old Blessing Okoro shot through a space-time tunnel that links a distant planet called Urth with Earth, arriving home precisely four months, three days, two hours, and eight minutes after she'd mysteriously disappeared.

Like children everywhere, Blessing had a special gift, and hers was the delightful one of *Breaking Rules*. Thus, despite being warned not to take anything home with her, she grabbed *Tales by Moons-light: Stories from before the Great Melt* and brought it, anyway. Then she hid it under her bed and promptly forgot about it. A strange amnesia settled over her, as it does over most children who return from an Urth adventure, and she didn't blink when her mother donated the precious cargo to the local library a few weeks later.

Years after, a thirteen-year-old girl found it there, thrilled by her discovery. She'd visited Urth, too, but because her gift was *Memory* she immediately recognized the book for what it was: a collection of old-time stories depicting events that happened before a catastrophe—the Great Melt—reduced Urth's land surface to a smattering of islands. Told and retold, Urth people passed the stories down through the generations, primarily by oral tradition, weaving fact with fiction until it was difficult to untwist the two. In some stories, animals talk to the people they love or fly through the vacuum of outer space with no air to keep them aloft. But the astronomy is accurate throughout, and children who are *Fascinated by the Cosmos* can confirm it for themselves.

The girl held onto the book, and, as she grew older, she began to select a handful of her favorite stories to edit for Earth children, adding facts as she remembered them, then illustrations as she remembered them, too, and then a glossary and pronunciation guide. In the end, her "Special Edition for Earth Children" included seven stories, each unfolding under the bright light of one or more of Urth's two moons, Lunera and Ru, or beneath the black canopy of moons-less skies ablaze with stars.

Stories feature a brilliant girl who outwits a sorceress; a young herdsman whose family's "curse" becomes a great advantage; a boy who saves his people from an ecological catastrophe; a maiden who uses her wits to escape from the clutches of an evil grandfather; a prince who exposes a wicked fortune teller as a fraud; a girl who overcomes a world of woes to gain a colony of "p-siders" that she loves; and two young people from opposing, warring lands who transcend the limited world view of each side to unite their peoples and start a life together.

On the surface, the tales are individual flights of fancy that offer a window into what life might have been like in another corner of the Universe, long ago. But they're united by interwoven messages that celebrate logical thinking and emotional fortitude with diverse young protagonists who struggle against daunting challenges and emerge victorious.